"How do I go about seducing someone?"

"What?" Luke looked at Vicky with interest. "What makes you think I know?"

Because you're the sexiest man I've ever met. "Because you're a detective," said Vicky.

"Right." Luke nodded wisely. "And in the movies us detectives are always getting seduced." He sighed. "I probably shouldn't be doing this, but okay, I'll help you. First you have to kiss him."

"You mean like this?" Vicky leaned forward and gave his cheek a brief peck.

"No! It's more like this." He brushed a finger down her cheek, slid his hand around to the back of her neck, lowered his head and kissed her right on the lips.

The second his mouth touched hers, 90 percent of Vicky's brain switched off, leaving her aware only of his warm lips moving with lazy ease against hers. He nibbled gently on her top lip, sucked in her bottom lip, then slowly, easily, unhurriedly slid his tongue between her teeth.

"Do you want me to show you what happens next?" Luke was breathing heavily, his hand on her breast. Her heart was beating three thousand beats per second.

"Thank you." Vicky scooted away from him, reminding herself that no matter how much she wanted to, she wasn't supposed to seduce Luke. "I, uh, think that's enough seduction lessons for one night."

Alyssa Dean adored writing *Manhunting in Miami.*
"I got the idea for this story by reading the singles
ads in the local newspaper," she said. "Someone
was looking for a man who was five foot nine, in
his late thirties, with black hair and blue eyes, a
nonsmoking good dancer who liked to fish and
enjoyed tennis and was good with computers and…
The list went on and on. My first thought was that it
would take a detective to find a man like that. Then
I thought what fun it would be for someone to hire
a detective to find them a husband." And thus
Vicky's story in the MANHUNTING miniseries
was born.

Alyssa and her family live in Calgary, Alberta.

Books by Alyssa Dean

HARLEQUIN TEMPTATION
524—MAD ABOUT YOU
551—THE LAST HERO
636—RESCUING CHRISTINE

LOVE & LAUGHTER
33—MISTLETOE MISCHIEF

Alyssa Dean

Manhunting
in Miami

Harlequin Books

TORONTO • NEW YORK • LONDON
AMSTERDAM • PARIS • SYDNEY • HAMBURG
STOCKHOLM • ATHENS • TOKYO • MILAN
MADRID • WARSAW • BUDAPEST • AUCKLAND

For Margo,
a great sister and a good friend

ISBN 0-373-25781-3

MANHUNTING IN MIAMI

Copyright © 1998 by Patsy McNish.

1

"MIAMI!" VICKY muttered.

She parked her car in front of the white three-story building that housed the main labs of the Oceanside Research Institute and slid out into the Florida heat. "How am I supposed to find a husband in Miami?"

There was no answer from the ribbon of ocean in the distance, the sandy beach or the lush vegetation surrounding the Oceanside complex.

Vicky reached into the car and gathered up her briefcase, her purse and an armload of books that hadn't fit into either, still murmuring phrases left over from the early-morning phone conversation with her socially correct mother in Boston. "You are thirty now, Victoria." "If you were here in Boston I'm sure you would be settled down with the right type of man by now, Victoria." "Maybe if you went out a little you'd meet someone, Victoria." "The family is counting on you, Victoria."

She shifted her load onto one hip so she could pull her identification badge out of her purse, flashed it at the security guard who opened the door to her building, and took the elevator up to the second floor. She didn't blame her parents for the not-so-subtle suggestions that she marry. It was just that finding a suitable spouse was a lot more difficult than she'd expected—and a lot more time-consuming, as well.

The elevator doors opened and Vicky hurried out. Not only were men hard to find, but she was getting tired of looking for them. She'd been trying to find one for almost three weeks now—giving the project valuable time that could well be spent doing other things—and she hadn't accomplished anything.

Her mood didn't improve when she reached her office and unpacked from her briefcase the latest report on the progress of her seaweed experiments. "Some progress report," she grumbled as she settled into the chair behind her scarred wooden desk. "I should have called it a Lack of Progress Report." That would be more accurate. She'd been working on this project for more than three years, and all she had to show for it was a truckload of underdeveloped vegetables. That was Miami's fault, too. She needed to spend every waking moment in the lab. Instead, she was zipping around the city, attending social functions she didn't want to attend in a useless effort to track down a husband in a city without appropriate husband material.

She was thumbing through the report and feeling disgusted with the world in general and this city in particular when her office door cracked open. Gina Wilson poked her blond head through. "You walked right past my desk without saying a word," she complained. "Either I've done something to annoy you, or something's wrong."

Vicky felt worse than ever. True, it felt as if the entire world was conspiring against her, but that wasn't Gina's fault. "Something is wrong," she confirmed. "But it's not you, Gina. It's Miami."

"Miami?" Gina opened the door wider and wandered in, a cheerful figure dressed in a fitted lime green skirt and a black short-sleeved sweater. "What's wrong with Miami? It's got perfect weather. Terrific beaches. Great vegetation and fabulous shopping...not to mention one of the best marine research facilities in the country."

Gina might have a point, but Vicky refused to be cheered up. "Miami might be great for sea vegetation research, but there's a real problem with the men here."

"Men?" Gina focused on the report in Vicky's hand. "The men in Miami are affecting the seaweed? That's the most amazing theory I've heard yet."

Vicky frowned at her. Gina might be blond, but she wasn't one of the famous dumb blondes who were the butt of those silly jokes. She was in her late twenties, with a body that even the self-absorbed male intellects at Oceanside didn't ignore, and a mind that contained a vast array of knowledge. She was supposed to be the admin. assistant for the head of the research facility, but in reality she took care of all of them. She could do a number of amazing things—soothe temperamental egos, retype budget projections so they made sense and even deal with the people in charge of office supplies. Her one fault was an odd sense of humor that Vicky sometimes liked, and sometimes found annoying.

Today she found it annoying. "Technically speaking, men have no effect on anything! However, it would help my experiments along if there wasn't such a...a man shortage in Miami."

"A man shortage?" Gina's jaw dropped. "You have got to be kidding. If there's one thing we're not short of in Miami, it's men. There are men of every type and

every description. Good-looking men. Ugly men. Men
with great butts and men with flabby butts. Men with
muscles. Men without muscles. Short men, tall men,
rich men, poor men." She smiled with obvious appreciation. "You just walk out onto the beach and there
they are, all lined up for you to look at. You pick out
one, go up and say, 'Hi,' and the next thing you know,
you've got a date." Her grin was wide, cheerful and
mischievous. "It's like going to the supermarket—only
better."

Vicky was so desperate that, for a moment, she gave
serious consideration to doing just that. Then she realized how ridiculous that would be and shook her head.
"That's fine for you, Gina. You're from Nebraska. It
probably doesn't matter who you marry."

Gina raised an eyebrow. "I imagine it'll matter a lot
to me...assuming I ever do something that dumb." She
gave Vicky a puzzled look. "Just out of idle curiosity,
why are we talking about marriage? I thought we were
discussing your research."

"It's the same thing." Vicky dropped the report,
sighing. "My sea carrot research is seriously off sched-
ule."

"That's not the end of the world, Vicky." Gina settled into a chair and gave her thigh-length skirt a
downward tug. "I'm sure we can all survive a few
more months if we aren't eating sea carrots. We can
probably exist on the carrots we have now."

"That's *not* the point. The world food supply is facing serious shortage. If we can use swampland to grow
actual food without injuring the environment..."

Gina held up a hand. "I know. I know. We could
save the world. But if we don't save the world this

month, we could do it next month. It will still be around, won't it?"

"It doesn't matter if it is, because I'm never going to have time to save it!" Vicky slumped back in her chair, depressed. "I should be working on this night and day. Instead, I'm wasting all this time trying to find a husband."

"A husband?" Gina's amber eyes widened to incredulous. "You want to get married?"

"Not particularly." Vicky could think of a number of other things she'd rather do, like take the midnight monitoring shift in the lab. "But I don't have much choice. I have to do it. It's sort of a...a family obligation."

"A family obligation?" Gina's arched eyebrows arched higher. "Getting married isn't a family obligation. Going home for a reunion when you'd rather spend your vacation on the beach is a family obligation. Visiting Uncle Frank who you haven't seen for a decade is a family obligation. Getting married just doesn't qualify."

"It does if you're me." Gina still looked puzzled, so Vicky went on explaining. "I'm a Sommerset-Hayes, Gina."

Gina's puzzled look intensified. "I know who you are. Dr. Victoria Sommerset-Hayes. But I don't see..."

Of course she didn't see. Gina was from Nebraska. How *could* she understand? "Sommerset-Hayes isn't just a name. It's a responsibility."

"Oh." Gina's lips twitched. "And I was beginning to think it was some sort of cult." She tugged her skirt down another notch, which brought it to mid-thigh.

"Go ahead. Tell me why your name obligates you to get married."

"It's simple," said Vicky. "My mother was a Sommerset and my father is a Hayes. I'm an only child. My mother has one brother, but he doesn't have any children, and my father is an only child. That makes me one of the last of the Sommersets...and the Hayeses."

"Ah." Gina's expression cleared. "So you feel you should get married and populate the world with a bunch more Sommersets and Hayeses?"

"I don't just feel it!" Vicky stressed. "It's something I have to do. I promised my parents I would and—" she sighed "—I can't let them down again."

"Let them down again?" Gina gave a little laugh. "How have you let anyone down? You're only thirty years old. You're working at one of the top sea vegetation research institutes in the country...and, as far as I know, you haven't done anything even remotely naughty. I don't think you've ever even had a parking ticket." Her eyes sparkled with excitement. "You don't have a scandalous past that you haven't told me about, do you?"

"Good heavens, no," said Vicky, horrified by the suggestion. "But I did move to Miami."

"You moved to Miami." Gina took a look at the wide expanse of city visible from the long window on her right. "That's not one of the top ten crimes in America."

"It is if you're me." Vicky pursed her lips. "It was bad enough that I studied marine vegetation instead of literature or art like everyone else's daughters. I made it worse by leaving Boston and moving to Miami so I could work at Oceanside."

"There's nothing wrong with Oceanside! We've got great labs, an outstanding staff." She gestured around the room. "And the offices are nothing to sneeze at, either."

Vicky followed the gesture, taking in the windows, the soft gray walls and the oak bookcases. The computer on one side of her desk was state of the art, and so was the equipment in the labs. "It's a terrific place all right. But this isn't the sort of thing that people like me are supposed to do." She twisted her hands together. She still felt guilty when she thought about her family's reaction to her "I'm moving to Miami" announcement. Her mother had spent a week in bed, her grandmother had dressed in black for days and her father had called three psychologists, a lawyer and the minister. "We're supposed to manage art galleries, or get involved in the country club or...something like that." Vicky didn't have much of an idea what her former schoolmates did to pass the time. She did have some friends in Boston that she saw when she went back to visit, but they didn't talk about their work. They talked about husbands and offspring and the theater...and a lot of other uninteresting topics. "Then we're supposed to marry well and—"

"And perpetuate the bloodlines?" Gina guessed.

"Exactly," said Vicky. "I didn't do any of the other things. That's why I have to do this. To make up for that."

"You want to get married to make up to your parents for getting your Ph.D." Gina made a face. "I'm glad I'm not from Boston. I ran away from home when I was sixteen, got mixed up with a member of a motorcycle gang and ended up getting arrested. Imagine what they'd make me do!"

Vicky gave her a disgusted look. "They're not exactly forcing me into it—although Mother does phone two or three times a week to see if I've met anyone." She sighed. "And she sounds so disappointed when I say no."

"I'm sure it will happen someday," Gina said briskly. "There are lots of men in Miami—and you did say you'd only been considering this for a few weeks."

There was an idea. Maybe if she left this for a while... Vicky perked up, then thought of her mother's reaction and sobered. "I can't wait for someday. I turned thirty last month. I have to get on with this before I'm too old to have children."

Gina shrugged that off. "You've got plenty of time. People these days are having children into their forties."

Vicky shook her head. "Putting it off won't make it any easier. Besides, the way things are going it's going to take me until I'm forty to find someone!" She sat lower in her chair, depressed. "I guess I should have started on this a long time ago. I just...wasn't thinking about it." She should have made it a priority—but she hadn't. If she thought about it at all, it was as a hazy event that would take place in the future—and she'd never given much consideration as to how it would come about. That had been a big mistake. "Now I have to find someone and I have to do it soon."

"I see." Gina's unwrinkled forehead pursed into concentration. "Well, if my experience is any indication, I'd say there's little chance of meeting someone at Oceanside. The men you run into here are either too old, too married or too obtuse to know us lovely females exist. Perhaps if you tried going somewhere besides your office you might meet someone—and I'm not suggesting the lab, either."

"I know what you're suggesting and I've been doing it. For the past two weeks I've done nothing but go out." Vicky listed her social events on her fingers. "I've been to three dinner parties, two cocktail parties and the theater." They'd all been hosted by connections of her parents, so Vicky had expected to meet at least one man with the right credentials. "Tonight I have to go to another one! And I know exactly how it'll turn out. I won't meet anybody. That's what happened all the other times."

"You haven't met anyone?" Gina's eyebrows came down. "What do you mean by that? You didn't meet anyone you liked, or anyone who was interested or..."

"Anyone who's...suitable." Vicky sighed. "I can't marry just anybody, Gina! The Sommersets and the Hayeses can trace their ancestry back to the *Mayflower* era. I can't mix that sort of heritage with just anybody."

"Of course you can't," Gina agreed. "What was I thinking of?" She paused. "So who can you mix this blue blood of yours with? Someone else who can trace their ancestry back to the *Mayflower* era, as well?"

"That's right," said Vicky. "And you would not believe how difficult it is to find someone like that in Miami!"

"It would be difficult to find someone like that anywhere!" Gina muttered. "'Hi, my name is Vicky. How far back does your ancestry go?' doesn't make a great opening line."

"I guess not, although it wouldn't be so bad if this

were Boston." Not that she missed Boston. She liked everything about Miami, but... "As a matter of fact, this whole thing *would* be a lot easier if this were Boston. I wouldn't have to find anyone because my parents would handle it."

"Your parents?" Gina repeated.

"That's right. They'd find a few men with the right qualifications. They'd invite them over. All I'd have to do is meet them."

"You get to meet them first? I thought maybe you'd be properly introduced after the wedding."

Vicky gave her a disgusted look. "Gina!"

"Well, you can't be serious. That sounds like an arranged marriage! People don't go around letting someone arrange their marriage for them in this day and age."

No they didn't, at least not in Miami—which was one of the problems with this city. "They do in Boston!" Vicky countered. "And my parents are quite willing to do it for me now—except everyone they know lives in Boston!"

Gina cleared her throat. "Yes, well, uh, things aren't done that way here."

"I realize that! It's too bad, too. It would make things a lot easier—and it wouldn't take up so much of my time. My research is starting to suffer!"

"Right," said Gina. "Your research." She gave her head a quick shake. "What about falling in love? Isn't that a consideration? I mean, even if you did track down Mr. Blue Blood, don't you two have to fall for each other?"

"No," said Vicky. Gina's eyes widened into shock and Vicky sighed. "Just finding someone is difficult enough. As long as I like him, and we have mutual respect..."

"Mutual respect?" Gina made a face. "You must want more than mutual respect! What about wild and passionate romance?"

Vicky had little experience with wild and passionate romance. Oh, she had dated a university professor from Australia a few times, and there'd been a Boston architect her parents had tried to set her up with when she was in her early twenties. However, she wouldn't classify either of those as wild and passionate romances. "Sommerset-Hayeses don't have wild and passionate romances. We marry people with the right background and a respectable career."

Gina didn't look impressed. "Gee, that sounds thrilling. Now I'm really glad I'm just a Wilson from Nebraska." She rose out of her chair. "I'm afraid I can't help you find this paragon of nationhood. I don't know anyone who's related to the *Mayflower* crowd."

"Neither do I," Vicky complained. She tapped a pencil thoughtfully on her desktop. "Maybe I should try a computer dating service."

Gina stopped on her way to the door and turned around. "I don't think a computer dating service would help. I don't imagine they collect information on people's ancestors." She chuckled. "You'd be better off with a genealogist—or a detective."

"MIAMI!" BARNEY complained.

He dropped his narrow, black-suited frame into a pale pink-and-gray chair at one end of Lucas Adams's office. "Hundreds of detective agencies in the city, and I end up working at this one." He gave Luke a mournful look out of his dark eyes. "Is it my karma or do I just have lousy judgment?"

"Neither." Luke peeled off his blue windbreaker and tossed it over the matching sofa. "You got sick of Chicago winters and wanted to come to Miami. I kindly invited you to go into business with me."

"And I took you up on it." Barney's mournful look increased in intensity. "I guess that answers my question. I do have lousy judgment."

"There's nothing wrong with your judgment—although I can't say the same for your taste in furniture." Luke wandered around the massive oak desk Barney had installed at one end of the office, and settled into the black hi-tech-looking chair. He'd made a major error when he'd agreed to let Barney handle office decor. All he'd wanted was a desk, a phone and a couple of filing cabinets. Instead, he'd ended up with a pink couch and chair set, oak end tables, a soft gray carpet and a bunch of glass shelving. "This place looks more like a brothel than it does a detective's office."

"No, it doesn't." Barney glanced around the room with a fond, proud gaze. "It looks impressive. And an impressive office attracts an impressive clientele." He paused. "After today, an impressive clientele would be a welcome change."

Luke sighed and chose a brown file folder from the pile spread across the desk. "You're not going to keep going on about that, are you? It wasn't a big deal. It's just one of those things that happen when you make your living finding people. Sometimes they don't want to be found."

Barney gave him a disgusted look from under his dark eyebrows. "There is a big difference between not wanting to be found and shooting indiscriminately at two innocent guys who are knocking at your door."

Good point. Luke struggled for a response. "No one actually shot *at* us. Robby just, uh, sort of aimed a gun in our general direction. It was more to scare us than anything else."

Barney didn't look appeased. "If that was his objective, he certainly achieved it. I was terrified."

Luke hadn't been too thrilled, either. He could still see the door of the apartment swinging open, revealing a hulking, six-foot-four gorilla of a man, his fingers clutched around a gun that had almost been as big as the guy himself. Luke had had just enough time to recognize the gunman as Robby Ingress, the twenty-one-year-old kid they'd been hired to find. Then the gun had clicked, the kid had started yelling... "I don't think Robby had any intention of shooting us. He was just defending himself. He thought we were thugs, come to collect money."

"Terrific," said Barney. "Now I'm being mistaken for a thug. That makes me feel so much better about myself."

"You might consider losing those black suits," Luke advised. "Black suits might be okay for Chicago, but they don't work in Miami. They make you look like a gangster." Come to think of it, Barney looked exactly like Hollywood's version of a gangster. He had a mop of black hair, eyes so brown they were almost black as well and a healthy tan. That, along with the dark suits he insisted on wearing, and his natural expression, which hovered between miserable and morose, made him look pretty darn sinister.

"There's nothing wrong with the way I dress. Unlike

certain people, I feel an obligation to add a little class to the office."

Luke made a face and focused on the contents of the folder. Barney had never been a fan of Luke's more casual approach. "We're not supposed to look classy. We're supposed to...blend into a crowd."

"Is that what you're doing?" Barney relaxed back into his chair. "Well, you're darn good at it, Luke. You blended right in with the crowd at the police station. It was almost impossible to tell the difference between you and the muggers."

Luke mentally groaned. Barney wasn't going to let this drop. There was plenty to complain about, he supposed. First there was encountering Robby and his gun. Then a passerby had caught sight of the action and called the police, who had promptly taken everyone in for questioning. Unfortunately, "everyone" had included Barney. "You used to be a cop, Barn. You should feel right at home at a police station."

Barney lowered his bushy eyebrows and glowered. "I was doing the arresting, not getting arrested."

"We weren't arrested! The police just wanted to ask us a few questions. And it turned out okay. By the time the cops arrived, we'd managed to convince Robby that we were there because his mother hired us to find him."

"Yeah, well, that doesn't—"

"Robby was all choked up about it, too." Luke grinned as he recalled the six-foot-four, two-hundred-plus-pound Robby going on and on about his mommy as the police led him out to the squad car. "He even thanked us as they were putting the cuffs on him."

"Right," said Barney. "I wonder how grateful his

mother is going to feel when she discovers that not only did we find her son, we cleverly had him arrested. Do you suppose she'll feel like paying her bill?"

Luke was already reading the notes he'd made about the next case. "You don't have to worry about that. We're not sending her a bill." Barney's eyebrows came down and Luke shrugged. "There isn't any point. She couldn't afford to pay it."

"She couldn't?" Barney's voice rose. "Then why did we take the case?"

Luke looked up. "Someone had to take it! Robby had vanished into thin air. His mom didn't know where he was." He pictured the small, frazzled-looking woman. "She's a single mom with three other kids, and she was so worried. I couldn't say no...and I'm sure you couldn't have, either."

At this point Barney looked capable of saying no to a roomful of Robby's mother clones. "That's just great," he grumbled. "We almost get killed and we don't even get paid for it!"

Luke wasn't too concerned. Money wasn't much of a factor in his life. That wasn't because he had a lot of it. He simply didn't consider it important. He wasn't in this business to get rich. It was something he was good at doing, and he liked helping people.

However, Barney sometimes saw things a little differently. "This is supposed to be a business," he lectured on. "People hire us to do stuff. We do it. Then they pay us for doing it. It's the way the system is *supposed* to work!"

"I know that. But—"

"You do *not* know!" said Barney. "You're a good detective, Luke. One of the best in the city. They were even saying so down at the police station. But you're a sucker for a sob story. You keep risking your life for cases that bring in practically nothing."

Luke winced and looked down at his desk. "Some of them bring in money." He couldn't think of one recently that had, but... "And I don't always risk my life. This thing with Robby was an exception."

"An exception?" Barney snorted. "It's happened three times in the past three weeks! Every time, the guns get bigger, the guys tougher. Any day now we're going to knock on someone's door and find an entire army of creeps, all carrying bazookas!"

Luke chuckled at that. "Hey, it's a living."

"It's not much of a living—especially when you refuse to charge people." Barney's tone softened. "We could do a lot better, Luke."

Luke knew what was coming, and tensed. "Let's not get into that. I—"

"We could," Barney insisted. "This is Miami, pal. There are zillions of zillionaires in Miami—and they've got mysteries to solve, too. Why, just the other day Suzette Harris called us. Suzette Harris, Luke. The wife of Harvey Harris. He's worth millions. She was ready, willing and able to pay us big bucks to help her out." He frowned. "But *you* wouldn't have a thing to do with it."

"Of course I wouldn't," Luke defended. "Do you remember what Suzette wanted? She wanted to hire me to find her daughter's poodle!"

"It wasn't a poodle. Pumffy's a papillon."

"Pumffy?" Did he really know people who had canine pets named Pumffy? "It doesn't make any difference what kind of dog he is. He's still a dog." Luke gestured toward the outer door. "Last time I checked, the sign out there said Templeton and Adams Investigations, not Ace Ventura, Pet Detective."

Barney folded his arms. "For the kind of money Mrs. Harris was offering, I could do a pretty mean Jim Carrey impersonation."

"Fine," said Luke. "Then why didn't you offer to do it?"

"I did," Barney retorted. "But the Harrises didn't want me. They wanted you. Mrs. Harris said Pumffy knows you!"

"Pumffy does not know me!" Luke had a flash of a silky-coated white-and-brown dog licking his hand at one of the Harrises' parties. "I might have...run across him at the Harrises' a couple of times, but—"

"That's a couple more times than I've run across him—or the Harrises." Barney leaned forward persuasively. "Look, I don't really blame you for not wanting to track down the pooch. I didn't feel like walking down the streets of upscale Miami calling, 'Here, Pumffy,' either. But there are other cases for the rich and famous that we could take on."

Luke looked back at the folder. "No, thanks."

"I'm not saying that's all the business we have to take. We can still do the runaway kid stuff. I know that's what you like, and I don't mind it, either. But that doesn't mean we couldn't take a few of the easier cases. The ones that pay."

Luke shook his head. "Not that kind."

"And it wouldn't be hard to get that business," Barney went on persuasively. "You seem to have all the contacts to do it."

That was true. Luke did know most of the members

of the Miami high-society crowd. It wasn't something he liked to talk about, though. "I haven't seen those folks for a while."

"They still remember you. Just this morning, Madalyne Flemming called to remind you about her party tonight. She's another woman who's worth a small fortune."

Luke didn't consider that any recommendation. He was fond of Madalyne, but that wasn't because of her money. "That's great. But I'm still not going to her party."

"Why not?"

"Because I don't want to." Luke gave up trying to get any work done and dropped the folder. "I don't want to get involved with that type of people again."

"That type of people?" Barney chuckled. "We're not talking about the dregs of society, pal. We're talking about the socially correct."

"Sometimes it's hard to tell the difference," Luke mumbled.

The room settled to silence while Barney studied him. "Maybe you've been in this business too long, Luke. You're starting to get old and cynical."

Luke straightened at that. "Two seconds ago I was a sucker. Now I'm cynical?"

"Okay." Barney blinked his sad eyes. "You're a sucker as far as the poor and helpless are concerned. When it comes to the rich and famous, you're old and cynical."

"I am not old and cynical!" Luke objected. "I'm only thirty-two. That's not old. And just because I don't want to get involved with those high-society types doesn't mean I'm cynical. It means I'm...I'm realistic."

"Nope. You're turning into a cynic. When Mrs. Harris phoned, you didn't even believe the dog was lost! What did you say to me? 'I doubt the dog has gone anywhere. Suzette's daughter is just looking for an excuse to get upset so Daddy will send her to Europe.' That's pretty cynical."

"You haven't met the Harrises." Barney raised a dark, heavy eyebrow, and Luke frowned. "Mrs. Harris has been to Europe three or four times because she 'got upset' about something—a 'missing' diamond bracelet that mysteriously reappeared after she got back, a decorator she wanted me to investigate because he painted the walls the wrong shade of green, her Mercedes that was 'stolen' right out of their garage..." He paused to chuckle. "Actually, that one didn't work. I stumbled across that car in a friend's garage two hours after Mrs. Harris reported it missing. She wasn't too happy with me about that one."

Barney still wasn't convinced. "That doesn't mean her daughter—"

"It does to me." Granted, he'd never had much to do with the Harrises' daughter. She was in her late twenties, he recalled, with a mass of auburn hair and a deceiving, wide-eyed expression she'd inherited from her mother. There was a strong possibility she'd inherited her mother's habit for losing things, as well.

"Luke..."

"I'm not being cynical, Barney, but...but even if I am, you can't blame me. You'd be cynical, too, if you knew all the stuff I know about that group." He did know a lot about them. He'd spent five years working for the Quade Agency—one of the most prestigious investigative agencies in the state. He'd become the "detective of choice" for the Miami crowd. He didn't want to do it again. "All they care about is their bank accounts, their possessions and their careers, which enable them to have their bank accounts and their possessions. When they're not acquiring them, they're talking about them!"

Barney raised his single line of eyebrow. "That's why you left Quade? Because you didn't like your customers' conversations?"

"No!" Luke raised a hand to massage the back of his neck. "I left there because I didn't want to work for those people anymore. It was a waste of time, Barn."

"A waste of time?"

"Yeah. You should have seen the cases they put me on. Follow around someone's husband to see if he's sleeping with the maid. Follow around the wife to see if she's sleeping with the chauffeur. Follow around the chauffeur because the wife thinks he's cheating on her while she's cheating on her husband. And all the time you're doing that, the daughter is trying to seduce you because her life's gotten a little dull recently!"

"You don't like being seduced?" Barney rolled his eyes. "You *are* getting old."

Luke gave him a disgusted look. "I don't mind getting seduced. I just don't like it happening to give some bored rich woman a cheap thrill."

Barney took a deep breath. "Just because Darlene was like that doesn't mean they're all like that."

Luke tightened his lips. "I wasn't talking about Darlene. I was talking about bored rich women in general." He had met several women who were like that. Darlene was just one of them. The big difference was, Luke hadn't realized that she *was* like that. He hadn't figured it out until she dumped him to marry a man twice her age, whose main claim to fame was that he had a bank account that would keep her in diamonds for life. Luke was well over her by now, but he wasn't dumb enough to let it happen to him again. "I don't want to work for people like that." He thrust his thumb in the direction of the window. "There are lots of people out there who really need help. I'd much rather spend my time working for them."

"You're still trying to save the world, huh?" Barney sighed. "I admire your attitude, Luke, but you're not being very open-minded about it. Just because people are well-off doesn't mean they aren't decent human beings. And it also doesn't mean they don't need a little help from time to time."

"To do what? Find a lost dog or follow around a spouse to see if they're having an illicit affair?" Luke shuddered at the thought. "No, thanks."

Barney raised an eyebrow. "It beats the hell out of getting shot at."

"That's a matter of opinion," Luke muttered.

Barney raised a rueful eyebrow. "What did I tell you? Old and cynical."

2

"I'M AFRAID I CAN'T HELP you there," said Madalyne.

She stood beside Vicky at one end of her lime-green-and-yellow living room, a short, square figure encompassed in a flowing silk caftan of much the same colors. "I don't know when William Blakey's ancestors arrived in America," Madalyne told her. "I just know that his father made a fortune in cosmetics."

Vicky wasn't surprised to hear this. Madalyne Flemming was a friend of a friend of Vicky's mother. She was a sweet woman, but she wasn't from Boston. That wasn't a character flaw, but Vicky had realized soon after she arrived that it meant Madalyne wasn't going to be much help in Vicky's quest.

"I could ask him if you like," Madalyne volunteered.

Vicky shook her head. "That's not necessary, thank you. I was just, uh, curious." She'd already eliminated William from her list of possible husbands. For one thing, he probably didn't know any more about his background than Madalyne did. For another, he appeared to be wearing some of those cosmetics his father had used to make his fortune. Vicky couldn't bring home a man who wore both lipstick and mascara. Her father would call *four* psychologists! That might help out William, but it wouldn't do much for her.

Madalyne put a hand on Vicky's arm. "Will you excuse me, Victoria? Harrison Bilmore and his wife have just arrived. I have no idea when their ancestors came here, but I really must go over and say hello." She bustled off with an air that bordered on relief.

Vicky took a thoughtful sip from the glass of wine in her hand while she watched Madalyne's lime-green-clad figure move through the crowd. At least the evening hadn't been a total waste of time. She now knew that lime green was the "in" color this year.

Apart from that, it had pretty much been a wipeout.

Vicky scanned the dozens of people spilling out of Madalyne's upscale, beachfront condo. Madalyne had told Vicky she was having a few people over. Instead, it appeared that she'd invited half of Florida. Madalyne had also claimed that some of Miami's most interesting citizens would be here. That was possibly true. So far, Vicky had been introduced to a number of artists, a couple of movie stars, a hairdresser and a lifeguard. Some of them were extremely good-looking, and could very well be interesting, but none of them were even close to what Vicky considered good husband material—or if they were, Vicky had no way of finding out.

That's because it was Miami! People here just didn't know anything about one another. Madalyne certainly didn't. She was a wonderful hostess, and she was trying very hard, but she barely knew anything about her guests other than their names! She certainly didn't know the important details, like when their ancestors had landed or who their great-great-grandparents were. If she didn't know, how was Vicky supposed to know?

Their appearances weren't any help. Take the pleasant-looking man at the other end of the room—the one talking with the blond woman in the brief, skintight blue-and-lime-green dress. He wasn't outstandingly handsome or expensively clothed, and he didn't have the best build in the room, although he appeared admirably fit with his wide shoulders and flat tummy. He was just a guy of average height, with an open, friendly face, and naturally wavy auburn hair that suggested he didn't spend hours with a stylist. Who was he? Where was he from? Vicky couldn't tell. His outfit of brown dress pants, a black T-shirt and a deep maroon jacket told nothing about his background, or occupation. He could be a thug here to rob the guests, or he could be a descendant of John Adams himself. There wasn't an easy way of telling.

Vicky took another sip and kept studying the man. The woman said something, and he grinned, a wide, tempting grin that lit up his face and crinkled his eyes at the corners. Vicky changed her mind about him. He might not be the best-looking man here, but she liked the easy naturalness of his smile. Up close, he'd be darn hard to beat.

Which meant he couldn't be a thug. Madalyne might be capable of inviting one over, but if she had, it couldn't be him. That smile, his aura of easy confidence and his relaxed attitude couldn't belong to a criminal.

They couldn't belong to a relative of John Adams, either. His attractiveness appeared to be accidental, as if he neither knew, nor cared, about his appearance. Aristocratic men were always concerned with how they looked—and they often were under the impression that they were a lot better looking than they really were. Besides, a relative of the famous Mr. Adams wouldn't hang around a lime-green-and-yellow beach-front condo in Miami.

On the other hand, she was here, and she could trace her ancestry back almost as far as John Adams.

Now she was being silly. Men that attractive were never the right ones. The ones she'd met in Boston were dull and unimaginative. But things were different in Miami. Maybe...

Her thoughts were interrupted by a swirl of green as Madalyne bustled up to her. "Victoria, darling!" Her round face was creased into a wide smile, and her gray eyes sparkled with excitement. "I've got someone here you simply have to meet. His name is Fielding Daniels...and he knows exactly when his great-great-great-grandfather came to America!"

WHAT WAS HE DOING HERE, how did Aimsly Woods keep her dress from falling to the floor and who was the classy-looking brunette in the cream-colored suit?

Luke swirled the ice cubes in his glass while he pondered those questions. The first one wasn't hard. He was here for two reasons. Madalyne was one of them. She'd called this afternoon in another attempt to coax him to drop by this evening, if only for a little while. Luke had tried to refuse, but she'd sounded hurt, and he'd felt like a heel. Madalyne was a bit of a ditz, but she was a kind soul, and she'd always been decent to him.

Then there was that "old and cynical" comment of Barney's, which had struck a little too close to home. Maybe he was a touch cynical about this crowd. After all, Madalyne was one of them, and he liked her.

She wasn't the only one he liked, either. He didn't

mind most of these people, although he did consider
the majority a little on the superficial side. They cared
about things he didn't think were important, like
money and prestige, and a lot of them didn't care how
they got those things, or who they hurt along the way.
As for their problems, well, those were pretty superficial, too, especially when stacked up against runaway
teenagers, deadbeat husbands and the host of other is-
sues that confronted normal, everyday folks. On the
other hand, there was a faint possibility that one or two
of them might have more serious matters to contend
with than a lost dog or a stray spouse. It seemed highly
unlikely, but even if they didn't, he owed it to Barney
to make some effort to draw in a few paying customers. He just hoped Barney wouldn't be too disappointed when business didn't pick up dramatically tomorrow.

He focused on the woman standing directly in front
of him. Aimsly Woods, daughter of shipping giant
Stanley Woods. The only problem Aimsly had was that
something—Luke wasn't sure what—had happened to
her old yacht and she'd had to replace it. And the only
thing interesting about her was that dress. It was one of
those casual, off-the-shoulder jobs, with no back and
hardly any front and it showed off Aimsly's size three,
bustless figure and smooth, even tan to perfection.
Since Aimsly insisted on punctuating her sentences
with a jerky bounce, Luke had expected the dress to
fall off her a long time ago. That hadn't happened. Either it was glued to her body, or there was a wire system that he couldn't see.

"...and then Daddy said he'd buy me a new yacht,

just like the old one," Aimsly was saying. "He had to have it specially made because I..."

Aimsly's dress didn't matter. Granted, she'd made it clear she wouldn't mind if he was around when she removed the dress, but Luke wasn't curious enough to take her up on it. For one thing, she'd probably talk nonstop through the whole event, which would drive him to the brink of insanity. Besides, he doubted that Aimsly's interest in him was anything more than curiosity and boredom. She might not be the most brilliant woman in the world, but she'd already figured out that a fleet of yachts couldn't be purchased on a detective's salary. Which would make him nothing more than a fleeting interest for her.

Just because Darlene was like that doesn't mean they were all like that. That was possibly true. However, Aimsly certainly was.

Luke's gaze fell on the brunette, and he forgot all about Aimsly and her dress. Now there was a woman he knew nothing about. She was around five-five, with golden brown hair that she'd sleeked into a clasp behind her head. Her cream-colored suit was so respectable it didn't stop until it touched her knees, but he could still tell that she had great legs...and the loose cut of her jacket didn't hide the fact that she had a lot more bust than Aimsly. Her skin was lightly tanned, suggesting she didn't spend a lot of time lying around in the sun, and her makeup was almost invisible. She had a narrow, intelligent face, and clear blue eyes that gazed around the room as if she couldn't believe she was here.

"Who is she?" he wondered.

He didn't realize he'd spoken out loud until Aimsly

surprised him by ceasing her monologue and giving him a curious look. "Did you say something?"

"I guess so." Luke gestured across the room toward the brunette. "I was just wondering about that woman. I don't remember seeing her before."

"Who?" Aimsly glanced over her shoulder. "Oh, her." She turned her attention back to Luke. "She's the daughter of a friend of Madalyne's. I think Madalyne said she was from the Bahamas. Either that or Brazil."

Luke doubted that. The brunette didn't look like someone from Brazil, and she didn't have enough tan to be from the Bahamas. "What's she doing here?" he asked.

Aimsly shrugged a bare shoulder. "I think she's looking for her husband or something."

Luke squinted at the brunette. It didn't look as if she was wearing a ring. "Did she think she might...run into him at Madalyne's party?"

"I don't know." Aimsly looked vacant as usual. "It does sound peculiar, doesn't it?" She jiggled and so did the dress. "But then again, you can never tell with these people from out of state. What was I saying? Oh, yes, my yacht. Daddy had to..."

She went on to describe the floorboards. Luke's gaze wandered over her bare shoulder to focus on the brunette again. She probably wasn't looking for her husband...but perhaps she was looking for *a* husband. And if she were anything like the rest of this crowd she only had one criteria—he had to have bucks!

Geez, that sounded cynical. Still, if that wasn't what she was looking for in a man, why would she be so interested in Fielding Daniels? She'd been talking to him for ten minutes. And now...now she was smiling at him! Luke's frown intensified. Why would any woman smile at Fielding? It certainly wouldn't be because of Fielding's personality, because he didn't have any. It must be his bank account—and she probably didn't care how he got that bank account, either.

Now that was a cynical thought, too. There was always the chance that the brunette didn't know how Fielding had acquired his wealth. It was a pretty small chance. Everyone in the room knew—with the possible exception of Madalyne. But since the brunette didn't appear to know anyone but Madalyne, it could be that she wasn't aware of Fielding's sordid business dealings.

If so, perhaps someone should tell her about them. Not that Luke expected it to make any difference. Still, she should be aware of what Fielding was up to before she decided to do something stupid—like spend the night with the jerk.

"THAT'S RIGHT." Fielding Daniels leaned closer. "I did say that my great-great-grandfather's cousin was from Boston."

"Oh," said Vicky. "That's, uh, what I thought you said." No, that's what she'd been *afraid* he'd said. "That's...fascinating."

"It's your family that's fascinating, Victoria." Fielding raised an overgroomed eyebrow. "You did mention that your mother was a Sommerset—from the Boston Sommersets?"

"That's right. She—"

"So your uncle must be Senator Wilson Sommerset?"

Vicky hadn't seen her uncle in years. "Well, yes, Uncle Willie is a senator. However—"

"And your father is Judge Luthan Hayes?"

"Yes, I—"

"Splendid. Just splendid." Fielding smiled, showing an alarming number of perfect white teeth. "I've always found that sort of solid American heritage to be a distinct advantage—especially in a career such as mine."

"Have you?" It hadn't done much for Vicky's career. "Exactly what business are you in, Mr. Daniels?"

"Oh, a variety of things," Fielding said vaguely. "It's not the sort of business that makes for good party conversation. Certainly not as interesting as your relatives." He curled a hand around her arm. "Why don't we find a cozy corner and discuss our common heritage? It could be that our ancestors strolled arm in arm into the New World."

Vicky stared down at his hand, resisting the urge to pull away. It was possible that their ancestors had met at some point. If they had, she fervently hoped that his had washed their hands before greeting hers. "I'd enjoy that," she said, although the idea of being in a cozy corner with Fielding made her nauseous. She finished off the last of her wine in one gulp. "But, uh, perhaps I could freshen my drink first." She held out her glass. "Do you think you could...?"

"Of course. You just wait right here." He gave her another predatorial smile, took her glass and strode across the room in search of a waiter.

Vicky released a small, relieved sigh as she watched him leave. *Forget about it, Victoria!* she ordered herself.

This is not the man you want to marry. You couldn't spend your entire marriage sending him off to fetch you drinks.

But was she being too picky? So he had grubby fingernails. So what? Apart from that, he was perfect.

Well, maybe perfect was a bit of an exaggeration. He was too tall. She didn't like the way he towered over her. He was also pompous, and boring, and he had too many teeth, and his eyes were too small, and every time he touched her she wanted to run screaming out of the room. How important was that? He had the right ancestry...and he was a businessman of some sort. Her parents would like those things. Granted, the idea of spending the rest of her life with him didn't appeal to her, but...well, maybe he'd take a lot of business trips.

"Amazing man, isn't he?" asked a male voice.

Vicky turned and found herself standing face-to-face with the maybe-thug-maybe-Adams man. He smiled his natural easy smile, and Vicky caught her breath. She'd been right about him. Up close he was darn hard to beat.

She realized she was staring and scrambled to recall what he'd said. "Pardon me?"

He gestured across the room with his glass. "Fielding."

"Fielding?" Vicky's gaze fell on his fingers curled around his glass. Clean fingernails.

"Fielding Daniels." He hesitated, then added, "The man you were just talking to."

Right. Fielding. The creep she was contemplating spending the rest of her life with. "Oh. Yes." Vicky cleared her throat and forced her gaze back up to his face. "What were you saying about him?"

"Just that he's amazing. You know. The way he can

carry on with his life." He raised his glass to his lips. "I don't think I could be that nonchalant if the grand jury was trying to indict me."

"The grand jury?" Vicky gave her head a quick shake. Why would a grand jury be interested in Fielding? Surely dirty fingernails weren't an indictable offense? "I don't—"

"Of course, I imagine he's used to it by now," the man chatted on. "After all, it's not the first time it's happened."

"It isn't?" Vicky said faintly.

He shook his head. "Nope. But they've never been able to make any of those charges of racketeering stick."

"Racketeering!" Vicky took a quick look across the room at Fielding. "Fielding Daniels is being investigated for racketeering?"

"That as well as income tax evasion, embezzlement, misuse of company funds..." He shrugged. "You name it and Fielding has done it. But he probably made a lot of money doing it."

"I don't care." Vicky gave Fielding's back a disgusted glare. No wonder he'd been interested in her father the judge! "I hope he loses it all when he goes to jail—or else has to spend it all on lawyers!" To think that she'd considered marrying him! The very idea made her shudder.

"I gather you didn't know how Fielding made his money."

"I didn't even know that Fielding had any money," said Vicky. "All I know about him is that his great-great-grandfather's cousin came from Boston—and

I'm not sure that's true, either. I had no idea he was a...a hood."

"Ah, yes, but a rich hood."

"A hood is still a hood." Vicky smiled gratefully at the man who'd saved her from making a major mistake. "Thank you for telling me, Mr...."

"Luke," he said. He held out a hand.

"Luke." It was a nice, normal name—a lot better than Fielding. "Victoria," said Vicky. She watched his warm, tanned hand curl around her own, and felt warmth curl around her lower body. *Don't get carried away, Victoria. You don't know anything about this man except that he's good-looking and charming and when he smiles his green eyes crinkle at the corners.*

They were great eyes, though. She was still staring into them when she heard a throat being cleared beside her, and a male voice said, "Your drink, Victoria," in a voice laced with disapproval.

Vicky tore her gaze away from Luke's and glanced to her right. Fielding was standing at her elbow, his small lips turned down into a frown. "Listen, I, uh..." She hesitated, unsure of the socially correct way of getting rid of a hood.

Fortunately, she didn't have to worry about it because Luke took over. "Ah, Fielding," he said. "Great to see you." He gave the other man a hearty pat on the shoulder that almost had him spilling the drinks in his hands. "Did Madalyne catch up with you? She was trying to find you."

Fielding didn't look as if he believed that. "She was?"

"Uh-huh. Something about your lawyer calling, I believe." He grinned cheerfully. "What's that all about? Another charge been laid in this grand jury thing?"

Fielding gave him a vicious look before turning a smooth smile in Vicky's direction. "I'm sure it's a mistake. However, I suppose I should check into it. You know how lawyers are." He handed Luke both drinks. "If you'll excuse me..."

Vicky watched him hurry away, then turned to Luke. "Thank you," she said. "I hope that's the last I see of him." Thank goodness she didn't have to spend the rest of her life with a man who didn't wash his hands. But it meant she had to start all over. "You don't think he'll come back when he discovers his lawyer didn't call him?"

"Don't worry about it." Luke handed her a glass of wine; his eyes sparkled with humor. "Fielding has so many lawyers that I'm sure one of them must want to see him."

This man was wonderful. Good-looking. A sense of humor. Clean fingernails. He'd even come to her rescue. Now, if he just had the right background...

Vicky was trying to rework Gina's "Hi, I'm Vicky, how far back does your ancestry go?" line when Madalyne materialized beside her. "Victoria, dear, whatever is the matter with Fielding? He practically bolted out the door!"

"Did he?" said Vicky. She raised her glass to her lips. "How...peculiar."

"Isn't it?" asked Luke. He grinned at Vicky over his own drink. "But then, Fielding has a talent for peculiarity."

Madalyne nodded agreement. "He does spend a great deal of his time consulting with attorneys—and he isn't even getting divorced." She patted Vicky's hand. "I'm sorry he didn't work out, but frankly, I believe it's for the best. I never could stand the man, no matter when his family arrived in America. I only invited him because we share the same hairdresser." She gestured at them. "Have you two met, or..."

"Sort of," said Luke. "We were in the process of meeting when you came along."

"Well, then let me introduce you. Victoria, this is Luke Adams."

"Adams," said Vicky. Wow. Maybe she'd been wrong about him. Maybe he was related to Mr. John Adams himself!

Madalyne was continuing on with her introductions. "Luke, this is Victoria Sommerset-Hayes. She's from Boston."

"Boston, huh?" He nodded. "I thought I recognized the accent."

"Did you?" He had white teeth that hadn't been reworked to look perfect, and a tanned complexion that wasn't overdone. That was good. Too much sun wasn't healthy. Luke looked healthy.

Vicky took a deep breath and crossed her fingers. "Where are you from, Mr. Adams?"

"Luke. And I suppose you could say I'm from North Dakota. That's where my folks are, anyway."

Vicky's stomach sank. North Dakota was almost as bad as Nebraska!

"Luke's our family lifesaver," Madalyne chatted on. "A couple of years ago my son, Eddie, was going through something of a difficult time. I called Luke and he sorted it out for me."

She beamed at Luke, who looked acutely uncomfortable. "I didn't do much, Madalyne. I—"

"You were wonderful." Madalyne's grateful look increased. "That's only to be expected, though. Luke is the best in Miami. Everyone says so."

Vicky was still coping with the North Dakota disappointment. "The best what in Miami?" she asked.

"Detective," Madalyne explained. "That's what Luke does. He's a detective."

"A detective?" Vicky's gaze went from Luke to Madalyne, then back to Luke again. "You mean like a...a private detective?"

"Sort of," said Luke.

"Exactly," said Madalyne.

"But...but you don't look like a detective." Her gaze roamed down his body. "I mean, you're not carrying a gun or—"

"Oh, Luke isn't that kind of detective," Madalyne put in. "He doesn't shoot people. He finds them. Among other things."

Terrific. The best-looking man in the place and he was a private detective from North Dakota. She'd known he was too good-looking and too interesting to be right!

Maybe it didn't matter. Maybe...

Maybe what? Vicky pictured herself introducing Luke to her family. "A detective from North Dakota?" her mother would say. Then she'd spend two years in bed. And her father...her father wouldn't just call a psychologist. He'd call an asylum!

Vicky gave Luke's good-looking face one long, last

look and turned her lips into a cool smile. "It was nice to meet you, Mr. Adams. Thank you for helping me. Now if you'll excuse me, I...I really must go check on my carrots."

3

VICKY WAS IN THE LAB the next morning, agonizing over her plant specimens and feeling generally disgusted with the world, when Gina wandered in. "Oh, here you are," she exclaimed. She rested a hip against the counter. "I've been looking all over for you. I was beginning to think you'd skipped out to search for Mr. Right."

"Well, I didn't," said Vicky. "I tried to find him last night and it was a waste of time. Again."

"You didn't meet anyone with the right ancestry, huh?"

"I did meet someone." Vicky thought of Fielding and shivered. "But he was a racketeer." Plus he'd been a creep. It was a good thing he had turned out to be a criminal. Otherwise, she might have been stuck with him for eternity.

"A racketeer?" Gina's eyes widened. "You aren't serious."

"Yes, I am." Vicky threw up her hands. "No wonder I can't find a husband here. It's impossible to tell the good guys from the bad guys without a program!"

Gina settled onto a stool and gave her customary short skirt its customary tug downward. It was lime green, Vicky noted. "How do you know this guy was a racketeer?" Gina demanded. "Did he look like a racketeer? Or is that how they introduced him? This is Mr. Criminal and he's a racketeer from the *Mayflower* era?"

Her amusement was not appreciated this morning. Vicky gave her a disgruntled look to let her know. "No, of course they didn't, which is too bad. If they had, I would have known right away. As it was, I couldn't tell. He didn't look at all like a racketeer—at least, I didn't think he did. He just looked like everyone else. I wouldn't even have known he was one if Luke hadn't told me."

"Luke?" Gina blinked. "Is he a racketeer, too?"

Vicky didn't want to talk about Luke. She'd had a hard enough time getting him out of her thoughts as it was. "No. He's a detective."

Gina propped her chin on her hands and looked utterly fascinated. "A detective and a criminal all in one night. This sounds like some party."

"It was...different." Vicky labeled a specimen and set the bottle on a shelf. "I think Madalyne had some of everything there. Millionaires...artists...lifeguards... criminals..."

"And a detective," Gina concluded for her. "What did the detective look like? Did he have a gun?" Her eyes glinted with excitement. "Was he there because the racketeer was there or—"

"No," said Vicky. "He was there because he's a friend of Madalyne's." She pulled out another slide to study, hoping it would take her mind—and Gina's— off the topic of Luke. "I don't think he had a gun, or if he did, I didn't see it."

"He might have had one of those shoulder holsters that they use in the movies," Gina advised. "What did he look like? Was he a Rambo kind of detective or more like the Sean Connery type of detective?"

"Neither." Vicky took a look through the microscope, but all she could see was Luke's image. She gave up her attempt not to think about him. "He didn't look like a detective, Gina—at least, not the kind they have on television. He was sort of...normal looking, in a good-looking way. He had auburn hair with gold highlights, green eyes and a great smile..." She sighed. "Real teeth. Clean fingernails."

"Clean fingernails, huh?" Gina sighed. "I've always been a sucker for a man with clean hands. This guy sounds like a real turn-on, Vicky."

"He was...pleasant." That was an understatement. "Unfortunately, he's also from North Dakota."

"Ah," said Gina. "One of the ancestrally challenged, huh?"

"I'm afraid so. Plus he's a private detective! A private detective, Gina. My parents would never approve of that."

Gina shrugged. "So don't marry him. Have a hot torrid affair. It might put things in perspective for you."

The idea of a hot torrid affair with Luke Adams made Vicky's palms sweat. "I'm a Sommerset-Hayes. We don't have hot torrid affairs." She focused on the last part of Gina's statement. "And there's nothing wrong with my perspective."

"I think there is." Gina took a deep breath. "Vicky, hasn't it ever occurred to you that you're looking for the wrong qualities in a man?"

Vicky's mind had been replaying her conversation with Luke. "What?"

Gina's pretty, perky face was drawn into serious

concentration. "I can understand you wanting to perpetuate the family line and all that. I just don't think you should do it with someone you don't have feelings for. People shouldn't get married because of their bloodlines. They should get married because they fall in love and want to spend the rest of their lives together."

"I told you. I can't—"

"And I don't think people who don't care about each other should have children. Wouldn't it make for something of a...a sterile environment?"

Vicky shifted uncomfortably. There wasn't a lot of affection between her parents...and it had created something of a sterile environment to grow up in. "That's the way we do things. We grow up in sterile environments and...and we get used to it."

"Well, I don't think you should pass it on as a family tradition." Gina stood. "This detective guy sounds perfect. He's good-looking and nice, and...well, just because he's from North Dakota doesn't seem like a good reason to reject him."

Vicky kept her head bent. "You just don't understand."

"You're right," Gina agreed. "I don't." She gave her blond head an indignant shake and turned toward the door. "I think the detective sounds like exactly what you need."

Vicky watched her tap out of the lab on her high heels, then turned her attention back to her work. Gina didn't get it. Falling in love wasn't the main issue. Sure it would be nice if that happened, but if it didn't, it wasn't that big a deal. The important thing was her parents. She loved them, and she wanted them to be happy. No matter how great Luke had seemed, he was out of the question. She didn't need a detective from North Dakota—at least, not *as* a husband. However, at the rate she was going, it might take a detective to *find* her a husband.

Vicky giggled at the idea, then paused in the middle of examining a particularly pathetic sample. "He's not that sort of detective," Madalyne had said. "He finds people." She was looking for someone. Maybe Luke could help her.

Vicky gave her head a shake and peered through the microscope. That was ridiculous. People didn't hire detectives to find them a husband. They hired them to drive around in fast cars and hunt down criminals.

That was on television, though. This was real life. Luke did seem to know a lot about people...a lot more than Vicky did. He'd be better at potential husband identification than she was.

Vicky replaced the sad-looking specimen and tapped her fingers against the counter. It was an outlandish idea, but it did have some merit. She sure wasn't having much luck finding a husband herself. Look how things had turned out last night. She'd almost got mixed up with a criminal! Even if she did meet someone she thought was perfect, how would she know that *he* wasn't a criminal, as well? He wasn't likely to bring it up, and the way things worked in Miami, other people might not know, or might not tell her. They didn't seem to consider those little details important. But if she had Luke check them out first...

Then there was the time element to consider. She could spend months on this project, waste hours of time attending social events while her carrots wilted in the lab and her parents grew more and more anxious. Sooner or later they'd loose patience with the whole thing, and increase the pressure for her to return to Boston and find a husband there. She'd feel so guilty that she'd give in. She'd have to leave her life in Miami, give up her research at Oceanside and spend her life in Boston talking about husbands and children and art galleries. The only thing that could save her from that was to find the perfect mate right here in Miami and to find him soon! If she kept on the way she'd been going, that was unlikely to happen. But if Luke was helping her...

Perhaps Gina was right. Perhaps a detective was exactly what she needed.

"I JUST DON'T get it," Barney complained.

He slouched his long body against the doorjamb, his mournful-looking face looking more mournful than ever. "You spent the evening at a party for the rich and famous. I spent it walking up and down the streets of Miami looking for a dog named Pumffy. How come you're the one who's cranky?"

"I am not cranky." Luke pressed a button to disconnect the cordless phone. "Geez, I hate these things. You can't even slam them into a receiver!"

"You want to slam a phone but you're not cranky?" Barney raised his single line of eyebrow. "What do you want to do to it when you *are* cranky? Have it taken out and shot?"

Luke started to glower, then realized Barney had a point and shrugged instead. "I'm not cranky, Barn. I'm...frustrated. I've been on that blasted phone all morning and I still don't have a lead on that Rysler girl."

"The Rysler girl?"

"She's a seventeen-year-old who ran off a couple of weeks ago. Her family hasn't seen or heard from her since." Luke held up a hand. "And before you ask, yes, it *is* a paying case."

"There's a nice change." Barney ambled into the office and dropped into a chair. "Is this case the only reason you're not Mr. Warm and Caring today?" He paused meaningfully. "Or are you still pissed off that Victoria with the two last names didn't fall at your feet last night?"

"Me and my big mouth." Luke could have kicked himself for telling Barney about that. He hadn't meant to, but this morning, when Barney had pressed him for details about Madalyne's party, Luke had impulsively told him about Vicky, as well. It hadn't been one of his better ideas. "I didn't want her to fall at my feet, Barn." For a few moments, he thought that's what she'd been going to do. When he'd first spoken to her, those clear blue eyes of hers had sparkled with interest. Then she'd discovered he wasn't one of the rich and famous, and the interest had vanished. "She didn't have to be so...so blatant about not doing it!" He frowned and tapped his fingers on his desktop. "You should have heard her. 'A detective,' she said. She made it sound as if I dug garbage out of Dumpsters!"

"Sometimes you do, but—"

"And then there was that carrot comment! Can you believe that? 'I have to go check on my carrots?' That's not even a good 'drop dead' line."

"Maybe she...has a big garden." Barney eyed him

narrowly. "Why are you so annoyed about it? I thought you didn't want women to try to seduce you."

"I didn't want her to seduce me—but I didn't like that carrot line, either." Luke thought about her soft curves and hesitant smile. Okay, maybe he wouldn't have minded if she'd tried to seduce him, although she hadn't looked like the type to seduce anyone. She'd looked a little helpless and a little naive and...

He gave his head a shake in a vain attempt to put some common sense into it. Vicky might look naive and helpless, but underneath she was like other women from that crowd. They were only interested in status and money. Granted, Vicky did have a few scruples about how they got that money, but... "How come you were out looking for Pumffy?" he asked in an effort to get her out of his mind.

Barney sighed. "Mrs. Harris called after you left yesterday. The dog hasn't shown up yet, and her daughter is beside herself. I said I'd see what I could do." His mournful look returned in full force. "I didn't see one sign of the pooch. You don't suppose he's been... dognapped do you?"

"It is a possibility, I suppose." Luke ran a pencil along his lower lip. Maybe he should check around— find out if...

What was he thinking? Pumffy hadn't been dognapped. The Harris girl just wanted Daddy to spring for a trip, that's all. He had a brief flash of a cute little dog licking his hand and shoved it ruthlessly out of his mind. He wasn't interested in Suzette, her dog or Victoria with the two last names. "No," he said. "If Pumffy had been dognapped, someone would have left a ransom note." He checked his list of contacts for the Rysler girl and picked up the phone. "I'm sure Pumffy is safe and sound and will rematerialize as soon as Harris's daughter has those plane tickets in her hot little hands."

Barney pushed himself out of the chair. "I'm going to check on it, anyway."

"Go ahead." Luke started to punch in the number of one of the girl's friends. "But it'll be a waste of time."

"You never know." Barney paused at the door. "Oh, by the way. That woman you met last night. You know, the one with the carrots."

"Uh-huh."

"I think she might be more interested in you than you thought."

"Oh?" Luke raised his head. "Why do you think that?"

"Because she called a few minutes ago." Barney checked his watch. "She'll be here in an hour to see you." He chuckled and wandered out the door, leaving Luke staring after him.

THIS WAS WHAT a detective's office looked like?

Vicky perched on the edge of the pale pink-and-gray sofa in Luke Adams's office and studied her surroundings. She hadn't known what to expect when she opened the door labeled Templeton and Adams Investigations, although her mind had conjured up a dark paneled room with wanted posters hanging on the walls, too many coffee cups littered across a desk and a cabinet full of guns. This clean, tastefully decorated area was a pleasant surprise. Luke couldn't be one of those television-type detectives who spent three-quarters of their time shooting people and blowing up things. He did other investigative stuff like finding people's lost necklaces or something. He wouldn't think it at all unusual to be asked to find her a husband.

Right. Women probably asked him to do that every day.

Vicky compressed her lips. Perhaps this was a peculiar thing to be doing, but what was the alternative? Doing it herself? She'd already tried that and it hadn't worked!

She focused on the man settling into the armchair at right angles to her. Luke didn't look any more like a detective than he had last night. He did look as good as he had last night, though. He was wearing a pair of brown pants, along with a beige shirt with the sleeves rolled up to the elbows, showing two tanned, strong-looking forearms. His hair looked as if he'd passed a hand through it a few dozen times, and he appeared more like a businessman who'd forgotten his tie than Rambo on a secret mission. Of course, detecting was a business for him, which, Vicky told herself, made him perfect for what she was going to ask him to do.

She just wished she didn't feel like such an utter idiot doing it.

She gave Luke a tentative smile. "So this is where you work, is it?"

"Some of the time." He stretched out his legs, looking comfortable and relaxed. "What do you think of it? It doesn't look much like a detective's office, does it?"

"Not especially." Luke smiled his crinkly-eyed smile, and Vicky practically melted on his couch.

"It's Barney's fault. He's the one who chose this stuff. I would have preferred something more... brown."

"Barney?" Vicky asked.

Luke gestured toward the outer office. "My partner."

"Oh. Mr. Templeton." Vicky took another look around. "Mr. Templeton did this?" She'd met Luke's partner when she'd arrived. He was tall and thin and sinister looking and she never would have guessed that he'd choose pink-and-gray furniture. That just showed how poor she was at judging people, and how much she needed Luke's help.

"It's hard to believe, isn't it?" Luke chuckled. "He might look like Al Capone, but his taste runs more along the lines of Madalyne's. I'm just grateful he didn't paint the walls lime green and yellow."

"So am I." Luke even shared her color preferences. Why did he have to be a detective from North Dakota?

Luke leaned forward and rested his forearms on his thighs. "So what brings you here today, Vicky? Were you just curious about the interior of a detective's office or..."

"Not exactly, no." Vicky eyed his bare arms and wished it was a social visit. "I've got a bit of a problem that I was, uh, hoping you could help me with."

"Oh?" His forehead furrowed into concern. "What sort of a problem?"

Vicky struggled for a way to put it that didn't sound completely insane. "I guess you could say it's a...a husband problem."

"A husband problem." Luke looked at her hands, then back up. "You're...married?"

"No, I'm not." Vicky drew in a deep breath. "That's the problem." Luke still looked confused, and Vicky didn't blame him. "You see, I need a husband. And I want to hire you to find me one."

SHE WANTED TO HIRE him to do...what?

Luke gaped at the woman perched on the edge of the sofa. She was dressed in a navy blue business suit, with a lacy, high-necked blouse peeking from underneath the jacket. Her hair was tied back the same way it had been last night. She looked cute and classy and old-fashioned, and there was that same aura of naive innocence about her that he'd sensed last night.

Was she really suggesting what he thought she was suggesting?

Vicky kept on talking. "I suppose it's something of an unusual request. But there are mitigating circumstances. You see..."

Luke listened, dumbfounded, as she launched into an explanation that involved Boston, the *Mayflower*, parents and something to do with seaweed. He hadn't known what to think when Barney had told him Vicky was coming to see him. Part of his brain—the cynical part, he suspected—had predicted it was because she wanted him to handle some trivial little socialite problem for her. However, the dumb part had been hoping that it was something else, that she'd changed her mind and decided that their mutual attraction was worth pursuing.

The cynical part had been correct. Not only wasn't she interested in him, she wanted to hire him to find her a man—and Luke was willing to bet that what she was after was a wealthy one.

"...and if that happened, I couldn't keep working at Oceanside," Vicky concluded.

"Oceanside?" Luke had been so flummoxed he'd missed parts of the conversation. "You mean the Oceanside Research Institute?" What did a research institute have to do with finding her husband? Had she hired them, too?

"That's right. It's where I work."

"You...work?" Luke peered at her. It had never occurred to him that she'd have a job. True, a lot of women in her social position did have high-powered, executive-type positions, but Vicky didn't look like a high-powered executive, and Oceanside wasn't a place where one of those would work. Perhaps she was there in some sort of fund-raising capacity, although... "What exactly do you do at Oceanside?"

"Research." Vicky's eyes sparkled with enthusiasm as she spoke. "My latest project is trying to grow a hybrid form of sea carrots."

"Oh." Luke took a moment to digest that. "Is that what you meant last night when you said you had to go check on your carrots?"

Vicky nodded. "Exactly."

"Well, I'll be damned." She hadn't been making up a poor excuse. She really had been obliged to go check on her carrots.

"I should have spent the whole evening at the lab," Vicky chatted on. "There's so much work to do. But I couldn't, because I have this...problem."

Luke had lost the thread of the conversation. "The problem with your, uh, carrots?" he guessed.

"No. The husband problem. I need one. That's why I went to Madalyne's."

Luke finally got it. "You went to Madalyne Flemming's party hoping to meet a man you could marry?"

Vicky flushed and bit on her lip. "Yes. Isn't that why most people go to parties? Single people, I mean. So they can meet someone?"

"No," Luke muttered. "Some of us go because our partners talk us into it."

"What?"

"Never mind." People did go to parties with the hope of meeting someone. Still, there was something about the way Vicky put it that sounded cold-blooded—almost as if she'd been on a shopping expedition.

"But the only person I met with the right qualifications was Fielding," Vicky continued. "I certainly didn't want to get involved with him—at least, I didn't after you told me what sort of man he is." She smiled at him. "I'm really grateful that you did."

"Are you?" Luke wasn't sure he felt the same way. She and Fielding might have made a good pair.

"But I don't want that to happen again. That's why I came to you."

Luke set his back teeth. This was almost as bad as having someone wanting to hire him to find a dog. No, it was worse. "We're not exactly in the matchmaking business, Ms.—"

"Vicky, please. And I don't need a matchmaker. I just need someone to identify the possibilities, so I don't have to waste my time doing it."

"Identify the possibilities?" He was supposed to line up his fellow men for her approval? "I don't think—"

"I don't even have that many requirements," Vicky went on. "I just need a man with a good, solid American heritage. Someone who can trace their ancestors back to the *Mayflower* era...and who isn't a criminal."

Was that why she wasn't interested in him—because of his ancestors? Or was it because of his bank account?

Luke waited for a moment, curious in spite of himself. "Go on."

"Well..." Vicky considered it. "He should be intelligent. And he needs to have a respectable career. My father would like that."

"Would he?" Now he was getting it. Not only didn't he have the right ancestors, but he had a strong suspicion that Daddy wouldn't consider private investigating a respectable career.

"I think that covers it." Vicky gave her head a decisive nod. "Although I would prefer it if he had clean fingernails."

"Clean fingernails." Luke couldn't stop himself from checking his own hands. They were in good shape. At least he had one of her requirements. Then he realized she'd left out one important factor. "What about money? Doesn't he—"

"Money?" For a moment Vicky looked as if she wasn't sure what it was. Then her expression cleared. "Oh. You mean, does he have to be rich?"

He nodded his head and she shook hers. "That's not important."

"It isn't, huh?" Luke wasn't sure he believed that statement. Still, she deserved the benefit of the doubt. "Let me get this straight. You want to hire me to get you a list of men with the proper ancestors, no criminal record, a good profession and clean fingernails."

Vicky's face colored but she retained her composure. "Yes."

"I see." Luke sat back and stared at her. Was this Barney's idea of a joke or had he just slipped into an alternate universe?

Vicky chewed nervously on her bottom lip. "It probably seems a little odd, doesn't it?"

"It is...an unusual request." And that was the understatement of the century.

"I know. But you can do it, can't you? You can find someone like that?"

"I suppose I could," Luke said slowly. It wouldn't be that difficult. There were plenty of men in Miami who were like that. Not that he was going to do it. It was everything he didn't like—a no-brainer case, a pointless waste of time, and there was no way...

Vicky's eyes filled with admiration. "Then you will help me?"

"Well, uh..." When she looked at him like that he wanted to do anything he could to help her, including throwing himself in front of a train. *No!* Luke took a breath and tried again. "I don't usually—"

"If you're concerned about the money part, you don't need to be. I can pay for your services."

Luke stiffened at that. *Stuff it up your ancestors, lady!* "That's not it. It's just not our usual kind of case. I don't—"

"Please," said Vicky.

She looked at him with those clear, guileless eyes, and Luke stopped talking. Her lips were slightly parted, her head tilted to the right, her forehead furrowed in concern. Her perfume touched his nostrils—a faint scent of lilac that reminded him of his grandmother. Something inside him went soft and mushy. She was pretty and sexy, and she seemed so honestly concerned about her family and so desperate for his help. It wasn't asking that much and...

Don't you dare, Luke! How many times had he got

caught up in something stupid because someone looked helpless?

A lot, but it wasn't like *this*. No one had ever looked at him and made him forget his name, his birth date and his common sense. He should stay far, far away from this woman.

He looked back at her, saw her anxious expression and swallowed. On the other hand, she wasn't asking anything impossible. It wouldn't take much of his time. If he sat and thought about it for half an hour, he could probably come up with a number of men who met her small list of requirements.

Luke, get a brain.

Then there was Barney. This was just the sort of case Barney had been urging him to take. Simple. Not too much work. Paid well. No shooting.

He had to be crazy to be considering it. But she looked so helpless and so worried. He could help her, and he could make Barney happy. Why not do it?

No, said his brain.

"Yeah, okay," said Luke. "I'll do it."

Vicky's face lit up, her mouth moving into a delighted smile. "You will?"

Look at me like that, and I'll do anything. Luke took a deep breath. Knowing he was being an utter fool, knowing that he was making a big mistake and knowing that he was getting involved in something he'd be a lot better off leaving alone, he smiled back at her and said, "Sure. I'll help you find a husband."

4

"I HAVEN'T EXACTLY MET someone yet, Mother," Vicky explained into the phone the next morning. "But I'm...close to meeting someone." She sandwiched the phone between her shoulder and cheek, and pulled on her panty hose as she talked. "As a matter of fact, I expect I'll be meeting someone any day now."

There was dead silence on the other end of the line, followed by her mother's excited but puzzled-sounding voice. "That's splendid, Victoria! But how..."

I hired a detective. Vicky rejected that response. "It's a long story," she said instead. She took a look at the old-fashioned wood-and-brass clock perched on the pine dresser that had once belonged to her great-grandmother, relieved to see that it was past time for her to leave. "I can't go into it now. I've got to get to work. I'll, uh, have to tell you all about it...some other time."

She winced as she hung up the phone. That had been an out-and-out lie. She had no intention of ever telling her mother what she was doing. Not that there was anything wrong with it, but she had a strong suspicion that her mother wouldn't approve.

Vicky wasn't even sure she approved. Yesterday, hiring a detective to handle this problem for her had seemed like a brilliant idea. This morning, she wasn't so positive. There was something about the concept that seemed…wrong.

That's how Luke felt about it, anyway. He had agreed to do it, but he hadn't looked impressed with the idea. Her mind went off on a little trip about the way he *had* looked, sitting on the armchair, his elbows on his knees, his chin propped on his clasped hands while he studied her. Great hands, with long fingers. His forearms were good, too. Solid. Masculine. As a matter of fact, his entire body had looked strong and masculine.

And his entire body was from North Dakota!

"That's quite enough of Luke!" Vicky announced to the quiet apartment. She jumped to her feet and stood in front of the mirror while she tied back her hair. She'd been tormented by little flashes of Luke ever since she'd met him, which was quite out of character for her. It was probably all this marriage talk. It must have done something to her libido. Granted, she'd never been a person with a lot of libido. At times, she'd even wondered if she had one. She didn't have any doubts now.

Which might be a good reason for her to cancel this project before it got started. She was obsessing about Luke, even though she knew he was unsuitable. If she hadn't hired him, she'd probably never see him again. Under the circumstances, that might not be a bad thing.

Except if she didn't hire him to handle this husband thing, she'd have to do it herself. Vicky made a face at her reflection. She didn't like that option, either. And what about her mother? The poor woman had sounded so thrilled at the mere suggestion that Vicky might meet someone. Think how happy she'd sound when this whole business was settled! It might make up for Vicky's unfortunate choice of a career and her move to Miami.

The clock chimed a muted dong, signaling the hour. Vicky gave an exclamation of dismay, snatched up her belongings and headed out the door. There were results to review, experiments to plan...intriguing, important things to think about. She pushed the whole husband issue to the back of her mind to worry about later.

She didn't think about it again until that afternoon, when Gina came into the lab. She propped a scarlet-colored hip against the counter where Vicky was studying root samples, and rested her elbow on the black Formica. "I hate to interrupt a genius at work, but Dr. Ridgeway stopped me in the hall. He's looking for a status report you promised him. I don't suppose..."

Vicky made a face. "I did start it...but then there was a problem with the fertilizer and I forgot all about it." She peered through a microscope. "I'll finish it this weekend." That was one good thing about turning her husband problem over to someone else—she had plenty of time to work.

But Gina didn't know that. "You can't work all weekend," she teased. "Shouldn't you be combing the city, looking for a guy in a pilgrim costume?"

"No." Vicky's attention was still on the root. "I don't have to do that anymore."

"You don't?" Gina's tone sharpened to curiosity. "How come? Don't tell me you actually *found* someone?"

"Not exactly." This was one healthy-looking specimen. She made a notation in her notebook. She might have just found the right fertilizer, but she wasn't leaping to any conclusions. "I've just arranged for someone else to look for him."

"You *what?*"

Vicky glanced into Gina's curious face and realized she'd revealed more than she meant to. Oh, well, she'd have ended up telling Gina all about it sooner or later. Besides, she was curious to see what Gina's reaction would be.

It wasn't good. When she'd finished explaining, Gina's amber eyes were rounder and wider than Vicky had ever seen them. "You really did this? You walked into this detective's office and...and hired him to find you a *husband?*"

Vicky gritted her teeth at Gina's incredulous tone. "Yes, I did."

"And he agreed to do it?" Gina's face was the picture of disapproval. "That's terrible, Vicky. You shouldn't have asked him to do it, and he shouldn't have said he would!"

Vicky remembered Luke's expression, which had been a lot like Gina's, and winced. "He wasn't exactly crazy about the idea but—"

Gina sniffed. "That's one thing in his favor."

Vicky wasn't sure she was doing the right thing, but Gina's attitude made her defensive. "There's nothing wrong with it, Gina. As a matter of fact, it's a...a logical thing to do."

"Logical?" Gina raised her eyebrows so high they almost disappeared into her curly blond hair. "You hired Rambo to find you a husband and you think it's logical?"

"Luke isn't the Rambo type of detective! And there's lots of logic in it." Vicky struggled to find it. "It's like...like when my car breaks down. I don't try to fix it myself. I take it to a professional. I'm not any good at fixing mechanical things." She took out the root slide and slid another under the microscope. "This is a similar situation. I'm no good at finding a husband so I've arranged for someone to find one for me."

Gina's voice rose. "There is a major difference between getting someone to overhaul your carburetor and getting them to find you a husband!"

"I realize that," said Vicky. "But it's the same principle."

"It is not! You're not supposed to fix your own car! There are only two or three people in North America who know how to do that anyway. But finding a husband...that's something you *have* to do yourself."

"I wasn't having any luck doing it myself!" Vicky objected.

"That's because you didn't give it enough time!" Gina put her hands on her hips. "You spent a couple of weeks at it. That's not long enough, Vicky. It can take years to find the right man. I've been dating for a decade and I haven't met anyone I want to spend the rest of my life with."

"You haven't?"

"No. Now granted, I'm not in any rush to get married, but the point is, I haven't met anyone I want to marry in all that time."

"That's not very encouraging. I can't wait for years to meet exactly the right person! And I can't keep going from social event to social event hoping I'll stumble across him. It's too...random." She returned her focus to her slide. "This way I can save a lot of time. I'll know he's suitable when I meet him."

Gina was shaking her head. "It won't work. You can't get someone else to pick out the man you're going to fall in love with."

"I didn't ask Luke to do that! I just asked him to find someone with the right background and a respectable career."

"The right background and a respectable career!" Gina gave a disgusted snort. "Those might be the qualities your parents want, but what about you? You have to spend the rest of your life with this guy. Don't you think you should be in love with him?"

The rest of her life? Vicky felt chilled. The rest of her life did seem like a long time to spend with a man whose only qualifications for the position of husband were his cleanliness and his bloodlines. "It's not like I'm going to marry someone I don't like. I'm sure we'll develop some feelings for each other."

"It doesn't work that way! Just because someone has a few superficial traits you think you want doesn't mean you'll fall for him." Gina leaned forward. "That's why people date. Because you never know who you're going to fall in love with until you do it." She paused. "Although in your case I wouldn't be surprised if you didn't figure it out unless it was engraved on a root specimen."

Vicky pursed her lips. "That's not true! I'd know it long before my plants did!" She didn't anticipate that happening—and she wasn't sure how she *would* know if it did. It wasn't something she'd ever experienced. She'd been attracted to a few men before, but she'd never felt that "in love" feeling movies and magazines espoused. Maybe it wasn't something she was even capable of feeling.

Vicky shoved that depressing thought out of her mind. "If I fell in love I'd be smart enough to know I'd done it. But we're not talking about falling in love. We're talking about finding a husband."

Gina looked exasperated. "It's the same thing!"

Vicky raised her chin. "No, it isn't. I need a husband with a certain set of criteria. That's what's important."

Gina scowled. "Are you telling me that if you fell in love with a man who didn't meet your criteria, you wouldn't marry him?"

An image of Luke's good-looking face flashed through Vicky's brain, but she pushed it aside. "No, I wouldn't. And I don't have to worry about that happening, anyway. The only men I'm going to meet are ones that do."

"Vicky..."

"Come to think of it, it's a good thing that I have hired Luke to find a man for me. That way, I don't have to take a chance of falling for the wrong person." Vicky gave her head a decisive nod and bent over her microscope again. "As a matter of fact, I think it's the smartest thing I've ever done."

"Well, I don't," said Gina. "I think it's the dumbest thing you've ever done."

"THIS IS THE DUMBEST thing I've ever done," Luke grumbled.

He stood in the crowded auditorium and studied his surroundings with a mixture of astonishment and dismay. Dogs. Everywhere he looked there were dogs of every shape, color and description. "I didn't think there were this many dogs in the world, much less Miami!"

"These are only some of the dogs in Miami," Barney corrected. "The crème de la crème of dogs. The actual canine population of the city numbers in the hundreds of thousands." He peered at the brochure they'd been handed when they came in. "Where do you think we'll find the papillon section?"

"You got me," Luke said, shrugging. "I didn't even know there was a papillon section. Come to think of it, I didn't even know papillons existed before you told me." He shoved his hands in his pockets and frowned at the crowd. "What are all these people doing here, anyway? Don't they have anything better to do with their time?"

"I guess not." Barney looked up from the brochure and scanned the room. "I think it's this way."

He wandered off through the crowd. Luke trailed reluctantly after him. "What exactly are we doing here?"

"I'm here because I'm looking for Pumffy. You're here to help with dog identification." Barney stopped in front of a cage containing a white-and-gold canine. "After all, you two are acquainted."

Luke made a face. "It's not as if we're close friends. I just saw the animal a few times." He took another look around. "And he looked exactly like all these other dogs. White with brown spots."

Barney rolled his eyes toward the ceiling. "That's because he's a papillon. They all look like that. But I'm sure he has a few distinguishing features."

"I can't remember any." Come to think of it, though, Pumffy's nose was a little different from these animals. And he had a way of putting his head to one side...

Luke gave his own head a shake. He didn't know anything about dogs and he wasn't going to recognize Pumffy even if he was here—which he wasn't. "Can't we forget this, Barn? Even if I could pick Pumffy out of a crowd, which I can't, I doubt that I'm going to run into him here."

Barney didn't move. "You never know. After all, Pumffy was entered in this show."

"That's probably why he took off." Luke glanced around the auditorium with mild disgust. "If I were a dog, I wouldn't come to something like this if I could find a way out of it. I wouldn't even have come here as a *human* if I could have found a way out of it."

Barney gave him an impatient look. "That's not the way a dog's mind works. Besides, according to Suzy, Pumffy enjoyed these things."

"Suzy?" Luke stared at him, amazed. "You call Suzette Harris Suzy? You're really coming up in the world."

"I don't call her Suzy. I call her daughter Suzy." Barney's lips moved into a hazy smile. "That's her name. Suzy."

"How original." Luke took in the dreamy, unfocused expression on his partner's face and felt a prickle of unease. Barney might be a tough ex-cop from Chicago but he knew nothing about Miami socialites. Getting mixed up with a Suzette Harris clone wasn't a good way to find out about them, either. "You don't want to get mixed up with Suzy Harris, Barn. If she's anything like her mother..."

Barney returned to earth. "There's nothing wrong with Mrs. Harris. And Suzy isn't anything like her, anyway. She's a sweet lady. Pretty. Intelligent. Good dress sense." His eyes glazed over again. "That's only to be expected, I suppose. After all, she did take a course in fashion design."

Luke couldn't imagine any of the Harris women taking courses in anything. "She did?"

"Uh-huh." Barney's forehead creased into concern. "She's some upset about Pumffy, you know. Mrs. Harris told me she's inconsolable."

"She probably is if Mommy and Daddy aren't coughing up plane tickets."

Barney ignored him. "That's why I'd like to find this dog as soon as possible. I don't think poor Suzy has slept more than two hours a night since Pumffy disappeared."

Terrific. Now Barney was feeling protective! Luke's unease increased. "Just don't get too attached to her. Daughters of rich men are only interested in other wealthy men. They can't help it. It's part of their genetic makeup."

"Suzy isn't like that!" Barney paused, then added, "And I'm not getting attached to her."

"No? In that case, why are we at a dog show, looking for a nonlost dog?"

"Because it's a good place to look!" Barney lowered his voice. "It's quite possible that someone took Pumffy to enter him here under a different name." He looked wise. "I understand that kennel records can be forged and fur can be dyed."

Luke stared at him. "You can't be serious! No one would go to that much trouble."

"They might. Pumffy was favored to win best of breed." He tapped his finger at a line in the brochure he was holding. "There's a sizable amount of prize money in that."

Luke leaned over his shoulder to check the figure, and whistled at the number. Money was a darn good motive. Maybe Barney was on to something.

"And it's not the dumbest thing you ever did, either," Barney muttered.

Luke was busy wondering how someone could dye a white dog so he'd look like a white dog that wasn't dyed. "What?"

"It isn't," said Barney. He compared the dog in the cage to the picture in his hand. "Agreeing to find a husband for Vicky. That's the dumbest thing you ever did."

Luke grimaced. Barney hadn't been impressed with that case, and he hadn't been silent about it, either. Luke couldn't say much in his own defense, since he thought Barney was right. Taking Vicky's case hadn't been a smart move. "It's an easy case that brings in bucks," he argued, a little unclear about who he was trying to convince. "That's what you wanted."

Barney squinted at the dog. "I didn't say anything about wanting us to turn into a dating service."

Luke flushed. "We're not turning into a dating service! I'm just finding a husband for Vicky. It's sort of like a...a missing person case." He glanced at the picture, then at the dog, hoping to change the subject. "This isn't him. Pumffy's nose is longer—at least, it used to be. I guess he could have had that changed with a quick visit to the plastic surgeon."

Barney gave him a repressive look and moved on to the next cage. "It's not anything like a missing person case! I've handled a few of those in my time, and I've always had something to go on, like a name, a description and last known whereabouts. And I've never put myself in a position where I'm introducing a woman I'm interested in to some other guy."

Luke imagined himself introducing Vicky to a potential Mr. Two Last Names and clenched his teeth. "I'm not interested in her...and I'm not introducing anyone to anyone, either. I'm just going to give her a list of possibilities. Men with good ancestors, respectable jobs and clean fingernails." Men that weren't him.

"Clean fingernails?" asked Barney.

"She likes clean men." The dog show faded into the background as a picture of Vicky, sitting on his sofa, earnestly explaining about fingernails superimposed itself on Luke's brain. How could someone who looked so sweet be so cold-blooded about finding a husband?

"Ah," Barney drawled. "I guess that explains why you've been washing your hands so often lately."

"I haven't been—"

"Yeah, you have." Barney chuckled. "I was starting to think you'd developed some kind of obsessive-compulsive behavior. Now I can relax, knowing that your problem is that you're just trying to appeal to our Ms. Vicky."

"I am not trying to appeal to Vicky! She isn't my type of woman."

Barney's dark eyes widened into incredulous. "You don't like the cute, sweet, innocent, sexy type?"

"Yes, I like that type," Luke said with exaggerated patience. "However, Ms. Victoria Sommerset-Hayes isn't that type. She hired me to find her a husband! That makes her cold and calculating, not sweet and innocent. She's another socialite, Barn, just like all the others." A little cuter than the others, a little more attractive than the others, but still like the others. "She's even got a typical socialite background."

Barney's eyebrows rose. "Checked into her, did you?"

"A little." The second she'd walked out of his office he'd been on the phone, finding out every detail he could about her. "She's from one of the most prestigious, influential families Boston has to offer. The Sommersets settled in Boston before it *was* Boston—and the Hayeses weren't too far after. Her father's a big-time judge, her uncle is a well-respected senator and the rest of her relations are just as upper crust." There were a few unusual things about her. Her education, for example. Most women of her upbringing didn't have a doctorate. That didn't change a whole lot, though.

Barney didn't agree. "That doesn't make her cold and calculating." He tapped his fingers against the brochure. "As a matter of fact, I don't think she is cold and calculating. I just don't think she knows what she wants."

"She knows exactly what she wants." And it wasn't him. Which was fine with Luke. His mind reverted back to the way she'd looked—classy and clever, and naive and helpless, all at the same time. There was something compelling about that combination, and about her clear blue eyes, her skin, her warm, luscious body...

Something too darn compelling—which was why Luke was going to stay away from her. Accepting this case had been a major mistake, and he planned on getting it over with as soon as possible. "I've already got a couple of guys in mind for her." They were exactly what she'd ordered. Respectable men with respectable backgrounds. A little light in the personality department maybe, but Vicky hadn't said anything about personality.

Barney looked surprised. "You have?"

"Uh-huh. I'll check into them a little, make sure they do have the background she wants, and pass their names on to her." He couldn't help but wonder what she planned on doing with this information. It was difficult to picture her planning an accidental rendezvous. On the other hand, Darlene hadn't had much problem getting to know Edgar Snow—especially after she'd discovered the size of his bank account—and he hadn't thought Darlene was the conniving type, either. "Then I'll be done with it," he told himself and Barney. "We'll get a nice fat paycheck—which should make you happy. Maybe that will make you come to your senses and stop looking for a dog that isn't missing. Then I'll be happy."

Barney still looked skeptical. "Right," he said.

"Trust me," said Luke, but he wasn't convinced, either. There was something about the idea of Vicky with Mr. Blue Blood that made his skin crawl.

IT WAS AFTER EIGHT when Vicky arrived at her apartment that evening. She shoved a vegetarian entrée into the microwave and watered her plants while she waited for it to heat. Then she spread her papers out on the kitchen table, propped her feet up on a chair and ate while she reviewed them. This was another good thing about handing the whole husband problem over to Luke. She could stay home and do fun things like this instead of having to hunt around for Mr. Suitable.

Of course, after he found him, she wouldn't be doing things like this—probably for the rest of her life.

Vicky frowned at the thought. Her conversation with Gina had gone a long way toward convincing her that she was doing the right thing. But that "rest of your life" statement bothered her. She'd been approaching this problem as if it was something to get over and done with—but there could be major ramifications if she did get married. For one thing, there was a good chance her future husband wouldn't want to set up house here. Her condo was a small unit that she'd chosen because it was close to Oceanside. She'd furnished it with items her grandmother had given her— a comfortable old deep green sofa with a mahogany back, an overstuffed armchair with wooden armrests, her grandfather's rolltop desk. She'd filled the rest of the place with plants, put a desk in the corner of the bedroom so she could work there if she felt like it and arranged the rest of the furnishings to suit her lifestyle. She liked it, but she doubted that her yet-to-be-named husband would feel the same way.

She stabbed her fork into the rectangular packet: He might not want to dine this way, either. A vision of her mother's elegant meals rose in front of her—a strong contrast to the way Vicky lived. She hoped Mr. Perfect wouldn't expect her to cook.

Vicky rose abruptly and cleaned up her few dishes. "He's not going to expect me to cook. I'm sure he'll be fine with caterers."

Still, the idea of a strange man changing the way she lived bothered her. "Don't borrow trouble," she advised herself. "You haven't even found someone yet. There's no point in worrying about where we'll live or who will cook right now. Besides, who says we have to get married right away? All I really have to do is meet someone. That would make my parents happy. We could have a long engagement. Maybe one that lasts for several years."

That didn't seem too likely. Oh, well, maybe Luke wouldn't have much more luck than she did. It wasn't that easy finding someone who met her qualifications. It could take him months to find the right man.

5

VICKY WAS IN THE LAB a few days later, reviewing her recent findings with a colleague, when Gina tapped her on the shoulder. "I'm sorry to interrupt but there's a man here to see you."

"A man?"

"A good-looking man," Gina amended. "He's got great shoulders, green eyes, brown hair." She arched an eyebrow. "His name is Luke Adams."

"Luke?" Vicky felt an unusual rush of anticipation at the idea of seeing him again. "Luke's here?"

"Uh-huh." Gina's eyes gleamed mischief. "He's waiting for you in the reception area. I said I'd see if you could fit him in, but if you're busy..."

"Oh, no." Vicky jumped to her feet. "You'll excuse me, won't you, Angus? Luke's a...a friend of mine. I, uh, promised to show him around and...and, uh..."

Angus Metcalf surprised her by beaming approval from behind his wire-rimmed glasses. "You go right ahead, Victoria. It's good to know that you've got something else in your life. Research is fine and well, but you should be thinking about settling down—and passing on your excellent scientific mind to future generations."

"Right," Vicky murmured. Angus was a genetic specialist so she should have expected him to say something like that. Still, his attitude made her feel more pressured than ever to find a husband. "That's just wonderful," she complained to Gina as they left the office. "Now my colleagues are trying to marry me off, too."

Gina patted her shoulder. "They might not have to wait too long. Maybe Luke's here to tell you he's found someone, although I don't know why you'd want to find someone when he's so yummy himself."

"You know perfectly well why. He's—"

"I know, I know. A detective from North Dakota." They turned the corner to the reception area. "But he's a real sweetheart, Vicky."

He certainly was. He was sprawled in an orange chair in front of Gina's desk, leafing through a magazine, looking casual and relaxed and absolutely delicious. He looked up when they turned the corner, smiled his crinkly-eyed smile and stretched to his feet. "Hi, Vicky," he said.

Vicky swallowed and tried for a cool, professional smile. In spite of her efforts, her voice came out soft and husky. "Hi."

"I was in the area and took a chance that you might have time to see me. Gina said she'd try to track you down. I gather she did." He smiled at Gina over Vicky's head. "Thanks, Gina."

"Anytime, Luke," Gina breathed.

Vicky watched them gaze at each other and felt an almost irresistible urge to bury them both up to their necks in lime-enriched soil. It was a ridiculous reaction, of course. It was only natural that they'd be attracted to each other. Gina was gorgeous and so was Luke and she wasn't interested in him herself and...

She gestured toward her office. "We can talk in here."

"Okay." Luke gave Gina another smile and followed Vicky into her office. He stopped inside the door and glanced around. "This is where you do your carrot research?"

"Some of it." Vicky closed the door against Gina's curious gaze. "It doesn't look much like a research office, does it?"

Luke grinned over his shoulder. "Not really, but then again, I've never been in a research office that wasn't a crime scene."

"I don't do a lot of work in here. I spend most of my time in the lab...or out at our research station in PalmGrove Point. That's where we do the fieldwork."

"Fieldwork?"

"After we get things going in the lab, we try to test them in as real an environment as possible."

Luke looked so interested that Vicky took him down to the lab and showed him around. He peered at her experiments and asked questions, and by the time they returned to her office she was more drawn to him than ever.

"You really like this stuff, don't you?" he asked when they returned to her office.

"Oh, yes. It's fascinating work." *But not as fascinating as you.* She watched him settle into a chair and stretch out his legs. His questions had been thoughtful and intelligent, and not at all what she expected. He was a clever man. How had he ended up as a detective? What did he do all day? Did he have a girlfriend and, if so, what was she like?

That's none of your business, Victoria! You're not inter-

ested in Luke Adams or his girlfriends! "I'm sure you didn't come here to discuss my work."

"What? Oh, no, no, I didn't." He stuck his hand into his inside jacket pocket and pulled out a folded brown envelope. "I came by to tell you that I've found someone that, uh, seems to meet your qualifications."

"Already?"

Luke nodded and Vicky's stomach lurched. There was no reason for that reaction. This was good news. This was what she needed. Besides, maybe another man would take her mind off this one. As long as he was in favor of a long engagement...

Luke slid a couple of sheets of paper out of the envelope and bent his head to read from them while Vicky admired his cranial structure. "His name is Jeremy Arabesct. He's an executive in the shipping business, thirty-seven years old and comes from an old American family." He looked up at her and grinned. "And I understand he takes a lot of showers."

"What about the top of his head?" asked Vicky.

"What?"

Now she was getting turned on by the top of a man's head! *Get a grip, Victoria.* "I was just, uh, wondering if he had dandruff," she improvised.

Luke chuckled. "I wouldn't think so." He passed the papers across the desk to Vicky. "Not with the number of showers he takes."

Vicky scanned the typed pages, impressed. She hadn't expected more than a name and a brief biography. Luke had provided all that, and more. Age, height, weight, birth date and birth order were followed by a family history, the fact that he had no prior arrests, a list of hobbies, favorite color, what he studied in school, the marks he'd gotten at university... She looked up. "How on earth did you get all this information?"

Luke shrugged. "I asked around. And it does help that I know the man."

Vicky knew people, too, but she didn't know this much about them. She didn't know this much about herself!

She focused back on the page. There was even a head-and-shoulder photograph stapled to the upper left-hand corner of the page. It showed a brown-haired, serious-expressioned man who reminded Vicky of her friends' husbands back in Boston. "What about the picture? How did you..."

"A camera and a telephoto lens." Luke flashed a brief, almost sheepish smile. "It's probably overkill on a case like this, but I thought it might help. Besides, it's a habit you get into when you do surveillance."

A habit to Vicky was getting home late and eating microwave dinners. Surveillance sounded dark and dangerous, and not the sort of activity she associated with the pleasant, friendly man seated on the other side of her desk. "When did you do surveillance?"

"I still do it off and on. And I did a lot of it when I was working undercover in Chicago."

Vicky gaped at him. "I thought you said you were from North Dakota."

"I am. I just took a roundabout route to get here."

"It sounds like it." It also sounded like something from a movie. Maybe she *had* hired Rambo to find her a husband.

"So?" Luke prompted. "What do you think?"

"Think?" She thought he was the most unusual man

she'd ever met. No, make that the most unusual *person* she'd ever met. She wanted to know more about him—everything about him. Who he'd done this undercover surveillance for. Why he'd done it. How he'd got into it in the first place. Why—

"About Jeremy," Luke encouraged. "What do you think about Jeremy?"

Right. Jeremy. Vicky smashed back into reality. Jeremy was the man she should be curious about, not Luke. She focused on the photograph, and tried to summon up some interest in the subject. It wasn't easy. Next to Luke, Jeremy looked bland and insipid and there was no way those narrow lips would speak words such as surveillance and undercover.

Which was exactly the sort of man she wanted. She'd never have to say to her parents, "Jeremy did a little surveillance work when he was undercover." Instead, she'd say, "Jeremy is in shipping."

She suppressed an inexplicable urge to yawn and read a few more lines of the report. Jeremy seemed to have everything she'd asked for—and nothing else. "He does sound perfect," she admitted at last. Too perfect. An uninspiring perfect. "Why isn't he already married?"

Luke made a helpless gesture with his hands. "That I don't know. Rumor has it that he's never found a woman his parents approve of."

Maybe they wouldn't approve of her. Maybe...

Luke dispelled that notion. "But I'm sure they'll approve of you. So will Jeremy. He likes the old-fashioned type."

The old-fashioned type? Vicky's spine stiffened at that. She was the old-fashioned type?

Luke rose from his chair. "I think that's it. Anything else you want to know should be in there. If it isn't, give me a call."

"I will." Vicky stood as well, still flummoxed by that old-fashioned remark. She worked in a pretty futuristic industry. How could she be the old-fashioned type? "Thanks for stopping by."

"Thank you for the tour." Luke headed for the door. "Let me know how it turns out."

"I will. I... " She suddenly realized he was about to leave and that she didn't know what was going to happen next. "Just a minute. Let you know how what turns out?"

Luke stopped with his hand on the doorknob and turned around. "You and Jeremy."

He was just going to hand her a few pieces of paper and leave? "But...but I haven't even met him yet."

"You should," Luke advised. "I believe that's one of the requirements of marrying someone—that you have to meet them first." He grinned cheerfully. "I don't know much about it, of course, but I'd guess it would be difficult to get a man to propose if he doesn't even know you exist."

"Of course I have to meet him!" Vicky snapped. She twisted her fingers together. "I was just wondering how I would, uh, go about doing that."

Luke looked blank. "Beats me. Go someplace he goes, I suppose."

That wasn't much help. "And then what?"

"And then...meet him." Luke shoved his hands into his pockets and frowned. "Don't you have some sort of a...a plan for this?"

"A plan?" Vicky shook her head. "No."

Luke rolled his eyes. "You should have! You did hire me to find someone like this. What did you think was going to happen after I did?"

Vicky flushed. "I hadn't exactly got that far."

Luke gaped at her. "You hadn't got that far?"

"No, I hadn't!" He compressed his lips and Vicky felt like throwing something at him. "You don't need to look so disapproving about it. In Boston, these things are...handled."

"Handled?" Luke looked confused. "Who handles them?"

"My parents!" Vicky exclaimed. "They'd decide who was suitable. They'd invite him over...or arrange for one of their friends to invite him over. I wouldn't have to do much more than dress properly and show up. And my mother would help me with that."

"Right," said Luke. "Dress properly and show up." His lips twitched. "Well, I'm afraid you're going to have to do a little more than that in Miami."

"I realize that!" Vicky sat back down. She might realize it, but she wasn't sure what *it* was. "What, uh, do you suggest I do?"

Luke shrugged. "I don't know. How do you usually meet men?"

"I don't," said Vicky. "That's why I hired you."

Luke stared at her. "You didn't hire me to help you meet him! You just asked me to identify potential suitors. What you do with that information is up to you."

What was she *supposed* to do with it? "You must have some ideas how I should go about—"

"I don't," Luke said flatly. "I'm a detective, not a dating service."

The room settled into silence while she looked at him

and he looked stubborn. "I thought you were going to help me with this," Vicky complained.

He shrugged. "I did what you hired me to do."

Vicky raised her chin. "You certainly did not." Technically, he had done everything she'd wanted, but Vicky wasn't going to admit it. She hadn't hired him to stand in her office and make her feel like a limp carrot, which is exactly what he'd done. She'd hired him to...to take care of this, which, apparently, he wasn't going to do. She had no idea what to do next. He must know something. A man like him had to know more than she did about it. Besides, his unconcerned attitude, along with that old-fashioned remark, had her seriously close to annoyed. She raised her chin and made a readjustment to her hair. "No, you didn't. You agreed to help me find a husband."

"That's right." Luke gestured at the papers. "And I've found a good candidate for the position."

"Maybe you have. But I can't find a husband until I meet him. You even said that yourself."

Luke suddenly looked uncomfortable...and just a little wary. "True, but—"

"So then it is part of your job to help me meet him!"

Luke blinked golden-tipped eyelashes a couple of times, then sighed. "You're pretty smart, aren't you?"

"Yes, I am," said Vicky. "After all, I do have a Ph.D. They don't hand those out to anyone who asks."

"I suppose not." He took a breath. "Look, I'm sure you'll run into Jeremy sooner or later. He hangs around with some of the same crowd as Madalyne does. If you..."

He stopped because Vicky was shaking her head. "That won't work. I don't want to go to a bunch more social events hoping I'll run into him. That was the whole point of this—so I don't have to waste a lot of time...socializing. Besides, I can't simply walk into a room and try to pick him up. We should be properly introduced."

"Properly introduced," Luke muttered. He bent his head and stroked a hand across his brow. "Okay. Well, uh, let's see. You must know someone who could introduce you. Madalyne maybe. Or—"

"Why can't you do it?" Vicky asked.

"Me?" Luke shook his head. "No."

"Why not? You did say you know him."

Luke looked acutely uncomfortable. "I just know him slightly. I—"

"Then I don't see why you can't do it. It would be a lot easier than involving someone else."

"Easier for you, maybe. It wouldn't be easier for me." His expression reminded her of how her plants looked when they were first placed in unfamiliar soil. "I find people, Vicky. I don't set up blind dates."

"I'm not asking you to set up a date! I just want you to arrange for us to meet. You could do that, couldn't you?"

"I suppose I could but I'm not going to. I—"

"Please," said Vicky.

Luke gazed into her eyes. His irises turned a darker shade of green, and interesting things started happening at the base of Vicky's torso. Then he released a resigned sigh and gave in. "Okay. Fine. If you want me to introduce you to him, I'll introduce you to him." He furrowed his brow and looked stern. "But after that, you're on your own."

Vicky wasn't going to worry about that part yet. "Of course." She gave him a grateful smile. "Thank you."

"You're welcome." Luke passed a hand over his face. "Barney was right. This is the dumbest thing I've ever done."

6

THIS WASN'T JUST the dumbest thing he'd ever done.

It was the dumbest thing anyone had done in the history of the world.

Luke sat in his office with the irritating cordless phone in one hand, and his head in the other. He'd arranged a number of assignations in the past, to get information, to put a child and a parent in the same room and, every so often, to track down stolen merchandise. Some of those had been darn difficult, and some of them had even been a touch on the dangerous side. Yet he'd rather do that any day than set up Vicky and Jeremy.

Luke had only been able to think of two ways of doing it. He could orchestrate a carefully planned, "accidental" meeting, or he could go for a more straightforward approach. After thinking about it for ten minutes, he decided on the straightforward method, simply because he thought it would take less effort.

Now he wasn't so sure.

It wasn't Jeremy that was the problem. He'd shown an uncharacteristic amount of enthusiasm as soon as Luke had mentioned Vicky's name. "A relative of the Boston Hayes family? Of course I'd like to meet her." And then, in a tone which made Luke want to break a nose, "How do *you* happen to know her?"

Luke had muttered something about being a friend

of a friend, which wasn't too far from the truth, and hung up, relieved that it was going so smoothly. Now all he had to do was get Vicky to cooperate.

"That's right," he confirmed into the phone. "It's all arranged. We're meeting Jeremy at seven-thirty tonight at the Carmel Glen Country Club."

"Tonight?" Vicky's voice was soft and distracted and a little confused. "Did you say seven-thirty tonight?"

"Uh-huh." It was a ridiculous thing to be doing, and Luke wanted it over and done with as soon as possible. "Is that a problem?"

"I guess not," Vicky said with obvious reluctance. "As long as it doesn't take too long. My plants..."

Luke listened in astonishment as she went into a little discourse about a fertilizer mix she was working on. Even though he'd seen her office and her lab, and listened to her enthusiastic explanations about her experiments, he still found it hard to believe that someone with her background could be this involved in her work.

"...so I would like to get back here to make sure it's properly applied," Vicky concluded. "How long do you think we'd have to be there?"

"I don't know," Luke growled. "I've never done this before."

"You haven't?"

"No, I haven't!" His sister often tried to set him up with one of her friends when he was home for a visit, but Luke wouldn't have a thing to do with it. He made a mental note to be more cooperative next time she tried it.

"Neither have I." Vicky's voice turned thoughtful.

"It is only for drinks. That can't take more than an hour or so. I should be able to make it back to work by nine. Ten at the latest."

Luke held the phone away from his ear and stared at it. What did she have in mind here? Was she going to rush into the club, down a drink, give Jeremy a quick nod of approval and then run back to work? "It might be best if you freed up the entire evening," he advised. "Jeremy did mention something about us joining him for dinner."

"He did?" Vicky sounded surprised. "Why?"

Luke pictured her, sitting in her office, with that bewildered expression on her face. She often looked that way. It made Luke wonder how she'd look at other times—like in bed, for example. Did she look into a man's eyes and say, "What was that?" after they'd finished? Or did she jump out of bed, stark naked, and rush off to check on her carrots?

Both images were intriguing. "Why what?" he asked vaguely, his mind still in the gutter.

"Why did he mention something about dinner?"

Luke came back to earth with a thud. He wouldn't be finding out how she looked in a bedroom. He was introducing her to Jeremy and then he wouldn't see her again. Which was a good thing. He straightened. "I guess he thought we might be hungry. It's a biological function, Vicky. People who haven't eaten for a while get hungry. Didn't they teach you that in biology school?"

Vicky's sigh sent his brain back into the bedroom. "I know all about hunger, Luke. That's the problem I'm trying to solve. I was just wondering why Jeremy would suggest that." Her tone grew suspicious. "What exactly did you say to him?"

She's from Boston, do you want to meet her? "Not much," Luke reported. "I just told him you'd hired me to find you a husband and that I'd narrowed it down to him."

There was dead silence followed by her horrified exclamation. "You didn't!"

"Wasn't I supposed to?" Luke asked innocently.

"Good heavens, no. You're not supposed to...I mean you shouldn't...you..."

Luke covered the receiver with a hand so she wouldn't hear his chuckle. "Hey, I told you I wasn't good at this," he defended when he'd recovered.

"I know, but I didn't think you were this bad at it! You're a detective. You people are supposed to be good at deceit."

Luke gave the receiver a questioning look. What was the matter with people? No matter what he told them, they insisted on believing he spent his life driving around in fast cars, shooting at people, telling outrageous lies and generally acting like a secret agent.

"Now what will Jeremy think of me?" Vicky concluded in that same horrified tone.

Luke frowned at that. She'd told him the whole story. Didn't she care what *he* thought of her? "I was just teasing, Vicky. I didn't tell him that. I just said that I thought he might like to meet you."

"Oh." Vicky still sounded suspicious. "And what did he say?"

"He said he'd like to meet you, too." That was an understatement. Jeremy had practically leapt at the opportunity. "Especially when he realized that you're related to Senator Sommerset."

"Oh," said Vicky. "Well, I haven't seen Uncle Willie in years."

She called Senator Wilson Sommerset Uncle Willie? Barney would really be impressed. "And he's heard something about your father, the judge. He said that he's one of the best legal minds in the state."

"He is a judge." Vicky didn't sound as impressed as Jeremy had. "I don't know about the 'best legal minds' part, but I'm sure he's very competent."

"It sounds that way." It also sounded as if Vicky neither knew nor cared about her relatives' reputations. That was unusual. Most socialites bragged about their connections. Vicky barely seemed aware of them. "I'll see you tonight then. Don't forget. Carmel Glen at seven-thirty." He was about to hang up when Vicky interrupted.

"Just a minute, Luke. You didn't tell me how to get to this Carmel Glen place. Where is it?"

Where is it? Carmel Glen was the most exclusive place in Miami. Everyone who was anyone had a membership, or wanted to have a membership. "It's Carmel Glen Country Club, Vicky. Haven't you been there before?"

"No, I haven't." She was sounding defensive again. "Why would I go there? I don't golf."

"Most of the people who belong don't golf. They just wear expensive golf clothes and look like they golf."

"Oh," said Vicky. "Well, I don't own any expensive golf clothes. And I don't have time to go shopping for some right now. I've got to finish setting up this next experiment." Her voice increased in excitement. "It's too early to draw any conclusions, but I think I'm getting somewhere. The preliminary results do look promising."

She sounded more enthusiastic about her experiments than she had about Jeremy! "That's, uh, swell," Luke muttered. "Listen, Vicky, why don't I pick you up? It would be easier than giving you directions."

"Could you? That would be wonderful. Then I wouldn't have to waste time trying to find this Carmel place. I could probably squeeze in an extra half hour in the lab."

"Right." Luke cleared his throat. "I'll see you around seven, then."

"Okay. Thanks, Luke."

"You're welcome." He started to push the button to hang up when Vicky interrupted again. "Luke?"

"Uh-huh?"

"What do expensive golf clothes look like? Do they have to be white?"

Luke mentally groaned. Did he have to dress her, too? What had she told him yesterday? *I wouldn't have to do much more than dress properly and show up. And my mother would help me with that.*

He probably did have to dress her. "No," he said. "That's tennis." He closed his eyes and tried to remember the last time he was at Carmel Glen, and what the women had been wearing.

He hung up ten minutes later, after helping Vicky mentally sort through what sounded like a limited wardrobe. "This is just great," he grumbled to the phone in his hand. "First I agree to find her a husband. Now I'm arranging blind dates, and telling her what to wear to them. What's wrong with me?"

"That's a good question," Barney agreed from the doorway. He ambled into the room and gave Luke a quizzical look. "I'm starting to wonder about you myself. Every time I come in here you're doing something weird with that phone. First you wanted to shoot it and now you're trying to have a conversation with it. Next thing I know, you'll be asking it out to dinner."

When Luke realized he was still clutching the handset, he dropped it as if it were on fire and made a mental note to start locking his office door. "I wasn't talking to the phone. I was talking to myself."

"That makes me feel so much better." Barney settled into a chair and assumed a serious, soothing tone. "Perhaps you should stretch out on the couch and tell me all about it? Then we can work on getting you the kind of help you need."

Luke glowered at him. "The day I let an ex-Chicago cop analyze me is the day I really do need help. And I don't need any help now. What I need is a partner who isn't a smart ass."

Barney chuckled. "No can do, pal. You're stuck with me." He raised a hand to tug thoughtfully on his bottom lip. "Seriously, Luke, it does seem that every time I come in here you're looking miserable. What is it this time? Haven't you found the Rysler girl yet?"

"I found her," Luke assured him. "She was holed up in a motel, without a penny to her name." There had been the usual tearful reunion scene that never failed to raise a lump in his own throat. "I don't know who was happier—her or her parents."

"Then what's wrong? Did her parents decide not to pay the bill?"

Luke shook his head. "No. They couldn't wait to

hand me a check." He didn't bother telling Barney that he'd tried to tell them to keep their money, but they'd insisted. "You found our little girl for us," they'd said. "There isn't enough money in the world to express our appreciation."

"Oh." Barney nodded knowingly. "Then it must be our manhunter, Ms. Victoria Sommerset-Hayes. What's the problem there?"

She wasn't the shallow socialite he thought she was, although she wasn't the warm and caring woman he wanted either, which was a good thing because even if he did want her, she thought he was her mother. "There isn't one." Luke lied.

"Didn't you say you'd found someone for her?"

"Uh-huh. She's meeting him tonight." Luke felt a pinprick of unease at that. He half wished he hadn't set Vicky up with Jeremy. Jeremy might sound good on paper, but in person he wasn't exactly Mr. Scintillating. Vicky hadn't asked for scintillating, though. She'd asked for well-off and respectable. Jeremy qualified.

"Ah," Barney drawled. "So that's what's wrong."

"Nothing's wrong!" Nothing that wasn't going to be fixed tonight, that is. Tonight, he'd introduce Vicky to Jeremy. Jeremy had sounded interested. Vicky had to be interested. They'd hit it off, and his brief stint as matchmaker—and Vicky's surrogate mother—would be over.

"You're sure?" Barney pressed.

"Positive."

Barney studied him for a moment with an expression of concern, then shrugged. "Okay, whatever you say." He started to rise, then sat back down. "Look, uh, if you're not playing matchmaker or looking for lost kids tonight, how about giving me a hand."

"Doing what?" Luke asked.

Barney cleared his throat. "The Miami chapter of the American Dog Breeders Association is having a wine-and-cheese tonight. Suzy thought it might be a good place to look for clues."

Luke gave him a disgusted look. "Ah, geez, Barn, you're not still looking for that dog!"

"Uh-huh," said Barney, not at all perturbed by Luke's tone. "How about coming along? You know a lot of people in town. You might be able to spot someone suspicious."

"Someone suspicious?" Luke shook his head. "Suspicious people don't go to wine-and-cheese parties. They're too busy robbing banks and extorting money to fit in these social occasions."

Barney pushed himself out of the chair. "You can't be sure of that. They could attend just to find out who has the most expensive animals—sort of an undercover reconnaissance."

"An undercover reconnaissance at a dog breeders' association party?" Luke gaped at him. "Where do you get this stuff?"

"Suzy suggested it." He beamed proudly. "She took a few psychology courses, you know. It gives her a real insight into the criminal mind."

"Suzy took psychology?" Luke asked, temporarily diverted from his own problems. "I thought you said she studied fashion design."

Barney nodded. "She did but she dropped it. I don't think it was challenging enough for her."

"And she probably discovered it was impossible to

meet wealthy men at a dress design school," Luke mumbled.

Barney's lips tightened. "If you don't want to help, you don't have to." He sighed and looked mournful. "Suzy and I will handle it."

Luke changed his mind. What the hell. He was already doing something ridiculous. One more ridiculous thing wouldn't make any difference. Besides, he didn't think Suzy and Barney should spend any more time together than was strictly necessary. "Of course I'll help. We're partners. I should be there to back you up in case a vicious dognapper mistakes you for a basset hound and tries to drag you off. What time?"

"Eight o'clock."

Luke did a swift mental calculation. By eight, he'd have introduced Vicky and Jeremy. They'd hit it off. Jeremy would ask her to have dinner with him. They'd go off together. Jeremy would be relieved that he'd finally found a woman his parents would like, and Vicky would be enjoying the fact that she'd found Mr. Acceptable. There was no reason why he couldn't give Barney a hand. "Okay," he said. "I have to go somewhere else first, but I'll meet you there."

"Oh?" Barney perked up. "Hey, if you've got a hot date..."

"It's not a hot date," said Luke, wishing that it was. "I'm just, uh, taking Vicky to meet Jeremy."

"You're *what?*"

"I told you. I'm introducing Vicky to Jeremy Arabesct."

"Oh?" Barney's eyes gleamed with curiosity. "I thought you said you weren't going to be introducing anyone to anyone."

"I wasn't going to," Luke admitted. "Now I am." He scowled at the look of derision on Barney's face. "Hey, it wasn't my idea."

"Then why are you doing it?"

"Because Vicky asked me to!" He'd known he should stay away from her. One look from those big blue eyes and he was toast. "I'd like to see what you'd say if she was sitting in your office, looking at you with that 'please, help me' expression." It wasn't just the expression. It was everything about her. She made him feel protective, even though he didn't want to feel protective and knew she didn't need protecting. It made him want to hold her close and make everything she wanted happen for her.

And what she wanted was someone else. *Don't go there, Luke! Been there, done that. You know how it ends.*

"I'd say no," Barney said with an annoying amount of confidence. "I was a cop in Chicago. Women don't get to me anymore."

"Right," said Luke. "That's why we're going to stake out a dog owners' wine-and-cheese. Because women don't get to you."

Barney frowned. "I'm not doing this because a woman asked me to do it. I'm seriously concerned about Pumffy."

"Yeah, right." Luke snorted. "Face it, Barn. We're both suckers."

"WHAT DO YOU THINK of this outfit?" Vicky asked the palm tree in the corner of her living room. "Do you think it makes me look old-fashioned?"

A slight breeze from an open window had the palm nodding agreement. "Thanks a lot," Vicky muttered.

She went back into her bedroom and studied herself in the mirror. There wasn't anything wrong with her pale green, knee-length skirt and cream-colored, short-sleeved sweater. It wasn't what Gina would wear, though. Gina would wear a lime green skirt that stopped just past her derriere, or one of her skimpy shorts outfits. No one would accuse her of looking old-fashioned.

Vicky pursed her lips and turned away from the mirror. She wasn't the long lean type that looked good in Gina-style outfits. Even if she put one on, she'd probably still look old-fashioned—or utterly ridiculous. "There is nothing wrong with old-fashioned," she told the palm. "Jeremy likes old-fashioned women. Luke said so."

Luke, however, had said nothing about liking old-fashioned women himself, probably because he didn't. What kind of woman *did* he like? Most likely the gorgeous, scantily dressed kind. That's what the detectives in the movies liked. Slim-hipped blondes with impossible bustlines and long tanned legs who looked, and acted, anything but old-fashioned.

"I'm being ridiculous, aren't I?" she asked the plant. "It doesn't matter what kind of woman Luke likes. What matters is what sort of woman Jeremy likes." She paused, then added, "And if I like Jeremy."

Now she was really being ridiculous. Of course she'd like Jeremy. She liked most everyone—except people who defoliated the rain forests and polluted the ocean, and she didn't think Jeremy did that. Maybe she'd even be wildly attracted to him. She picked up his picture and tried to imagine herself wildly attracted to the man in that photograph. It was a big stretch. Not only couldn't she picture herself being wildly attracted to him, she couldn't picture any woman being wildly attracted to him.

She set down the photograph. It wasn't fair to judge a person by their picture. Lots of people were a lot better in person than they looked through a lens. She fervently hoped Jeremy was one of those people.

She hoped it even more when Luke arrived.

He showed up ten minutes late, dressed in a formal-looking suit, a white shirt and a tie. "I thought you told me to wear something casual," she said as her eyes devoured him.

"I did." He glanced at his own clothes. "Don't worry about this. I'm going somewhere later and won't have time to change." He shoved his hands into his pockets and looked around curiously. "Nice place. Where did you get all the neat old furniture?"

"My grandmother gave me most of it." Where was he going all dressed up like that? More importantly, who was he going there with? *None of your business, Victoria.* She didn't care where Luke went. She would meet Jeremy and her thoughts would be on him. However, she couldn't help wondering what Luke's date would be wearing. It probably wasn't a respectable-looking skirt and blouse.

She smoothed her hands down her skirt. "Don't you think this is a little too casual?"

Luke gave her a quick head-to-toe assessment. "It's fine. A bit on the formal side, maybe, but it's the sort of thing that'll appeal to Jeremy."

But it didn't appeal to him? Vicky gritted her teeth. She didn't want to appeal to him, but he could have been a little more tactful about it. "Would you like a drink before we leave?" she asked. A drink would be good. It would calm her down...and maybe when she handed Luke his she could accidentally spill it. Liquor spilled over his pants would mean he'd have to go home and change, which would make him late for his date. Then Miss Not-Old-Fashioned would be annoyed and...

But Luke was checking his watch and shaking his head. "We'd better get going. Jeremy's extremely punctual. And I'm sure you're anxious to meet him."

"Of course I am." There was a good chance he was her future husband. Naturally, she was looking forward to meeting him. Maybe if she told herself that enough times, she would actually feel it.

She accompanied Luke down the stairs and out into the fading heat of early evening. There were a number of cars parked in the visitors' parking area. Luke stopped in front of a nondescript beige sedan and pulled a set of keys out of his pocket. "Is this *your* car?" Vicky asked as he unlocked the passenger door.

"Uh-huh." He opened the door and motioned for her to get in. "Is there something wrong with it?"

"No, of course not." The inside was clean, and, although it was an older model, it looked well-maintained. "It's just that, in the movies, detectives drive red convertibles."

"I know." Luke looked puzzled by that. "I don't know why they'd do that. Red convertibles are way too conspicuous. Detectives aren't supposed to be conspicuous."

Then why was he one? He'd stand out in any crowd. Jeremy, Vicky reminded herself. She was supposed to be thinking about Jeremy. "What's Jeremy like?" she asked after Luke had climbed behind the steering wheel.

Luke glanced over at her. "I thought I told you all about him."

"You told me some things about him. But you didn't tell me much about what he's like in person. I mean, uh, what should we talk about?"

"The usual things, I guess." Luke put the key in the ignition and switched on the car. "Golf. Tennis. The best stock to buy."

If that was all he could talk about, this was going to be a silent evening. "We can't talk about stocks," Vicky decided. "I don't know anything about that. And I don't know anything about golf or tennis, either."

"You don't?" Luke stopped checking the oncoming traffic to give her a surprised look. "Didn't you go to some upper-crust girls' school where they taught these things?"

Upper-crust girls' school? Did he think all old-fashioned women from Boston went to an upper-crust girls' school? "No," Vicky said very seriously. "At my upper-crust girls' school we weren't permitted to do anything that would make us perspire." She lowered her voice, confidentially. "Three girls were caught doing it once and they were immediately expelled."

Luke did a perfect double take. "You're kidding?"

"Of course." Vicky giggled at his expression. "I didn't even *go* to an upper-crust girls' school. I went to a public school along with everybody else."

Luke looked as surprised at that as he had with her earlier statement. "Really?"

"Uh-huh." Vicky grew reflective. "There was actually a big family row about it. My grandmother wanted me to go to some snooty boarding school, but my father didn't. He said it was a waste of my intellectual potential. And my mother didn't like the idea of me going away. By then they'd realized that I was going to be an only child, and they didn't want me to be away from home." She sighed. "Mother always felt it was her fault that I turned out this way."

Luke concentrated on driving. "Turned out what way?"

Vicky waved a hand. "You know. Living in Miami. Working in the scientific field instead of the arts." She entwined her fingers, her shoulders dropping at the sudden rush of guilt. "That's why I have to find the perfect husband. Maybe if I do, Mother won't feel so terrible about everything."

They stopped for a traffic light. Luke turned a quizzical face toward her. "That's really why you're doing this?"

"Uh-huh." Vicky watched the traffic go by. "It would be great if Jeremy worked out. Then I wouldn't have to feel guilty anymore."

The light changed. Luke focused back on the road. "Well, uh, I don't know about Jeremy. He is considered something of a catch, I suppose, but—"

"He is?" The man she'd seen in that photograph didn't look like her idea of a catch. Maybe he was better in person. "Why is that?"

"The usual reason. He's going to be worth a lot of money someday." Luke gave her a curious look. "That was in the information sheet I gave you. Didn't you read it?"

No, she hadn't, because she'd been too busy looking

at Jeremy's picture. "I...skimmed through it. I was amazed at how much you found out about him."

Luke chuckled. "I'm a detective. I'm supposed to be good at finding out stuff about people."

"I guess." Vicky shifted to face his profile. "How does a person become a detective?"

"Lots of ways. Barney's an ex-cop. Other people just...drift into it."

"Is that what you did?"

"Pretty much," Luke admitted. "It wasn't what I meant to do with my life. I started out studying social work."

"In North Dakota?" Vicky guessed.

"That's right."

"So how did you end up—?"

"Here?" He chuckled. "Well, I suppose you could say that it's Evan's fault."

"Evan?"

"My cousin, Evan. He's a chiropractor in Fargo now, but when he was a kid, he was kind of mixed up. One day he just...took off. I managed to track him down and talk some sense into him." He shrugged. "The next thing I knew, other folks were asking me for help."

He stopped and Vicky had to prompt him to continue. "Go on."

"There isn't much else. After I graduated, I started working in the family counseling area. That seemed to involve tracking down kids, too. I followed one to Chicago—that's where I ran into Barney. He convinced me to get a private detective's license. He said if I was doing it, I might as well be getting paid for it. After I got my license, Quade's offered me a job in Miami. I accepted."

"Quade's?"

"It's a detective agency here in town." Luke turned down his lips. "They told me I'd be doing the same sort of thing, but that's not how it was. I spent more time looking for people's lost wristwatches than I did helping families in distress."

Vicky spent a moment digesting that. "Is that why you're not with Quade's anymore?"

Luke nodded. "Not that there was anything wrong with Quade's. They were decent enough to me. I just like to do something that has a little more substance."

"I suppose that doesn't usually involve finding husbands for people."

Luke glanced over at her and smiled. "Not usually, no."

"I didn't think so." Vicky cleared her throat. "So, uh, why did you agree to do it?"

"Because you asked me to." He blinked down long, golden-tipped lashes, then glanced sideways at her. "Besides, I didn't want you to make another mistake and end up with a creep like Fielding."

"That's nice of you," Vicky said softly. She settled back in her seat and watched him drive. Nice was an overused word, but it was exactly right for Luke. He was a nice guy, with a social conscience. She liked that in a man. She hoped this Jeremy had one, too.

UNFORTUNATELY, JEREMY didn't seem to have much of anything.

He was in the lounge when they arrived, looking as serious and intense as he had in his picture. Luke shook hands with him, then performed the introductions. "This is Victoria Sommerset-Hayes," he said while Victoria studied Jeremy's beige-on-beige golfing outfit. "Vicky, this is Jeremy Arabesct. I believe I've mentioned him." He stepped back with a relieved aura that clearly telegraphed "over to you."

Vicky took a deep breath and gave Jeremy her best smile. "It's nice to meet you, Jeremy. Luke has told me so much about you." That was true. Perhaps one day she would tell Jeremy all about it and they'd laugh.

Or maybe they wouldn't. Laughing didn't seem to be one of Jeremy's accomplishments. He returned Vicky's smile with a pale, serious one of his own, gave her hand a brief, serious shake and took the chair across from her. "So, Victoria, I understand you're from Boston?"

"Yes." Vicky focused on the hand she'd just shaken. His nails were clean. So were his fingers, and his palms. She'd never seen hands that clean.

Actually everything about Jeremy was clean. He almost looked as if he'd been passed through a vat of bleach. It wasn't a bad thing, although she couldn't help comparing his blandness to Luke's more natural appearance.

Jeremy sat straight up in his chair and studied Vicky out of pale brown eyes. "You wouldn't, by any chance, be related to Senator Wilson Sommerset?"

Not Uncle Willie again! "He is my uncle. But I don't see much of him."

Jeremy didn't appear to have heard her. "Father would enjoy meeting the senator. We'll have to get together when he's in town."

Vicky couldn't think of a reason why her uncle would come to Miami. "I don't know when Uncle Willie would—"

"Perhaps he'd have time to fit in a round of golf." Jeremy raised a dull brown eyebrow. "You do golf, don't you, Victoria?"

Vicky shook her head. "I'm afraid not."

"That's a shame." Jeremy's forehead pursed while he digested this piece of information. "Although I suppose it is something that can be remedied."

It sounded as if he was fixing a carburetor! Vicky's spine stiffened with resentment. "I doubt it. I'm not very athletic."

Jeremy ignored that and concentrated fully on repairing what he obviously considered a major flaw in her character. "The golf pro here isn't too bad. Not a great talent, perhaps, but he could certainly get you started. And I'm sure Mother would take you out a few times."

Vicky gritted her teeth. Then gave herself a mental kick. What was the matter with her? That could be her mother-in-law he was talking about. Surely she could spend a few hours getting to know her? "That would be...splendid," she managed. She gave him a determined smile. She could like him if she put her mind to it.

Twenty minutes later, she wasn't so sure. It wasn't that she disliked him. She couldn't even muster up that much of a reaction. Her impressions from his photograph had been dead-on accurate. Jeremy wasn't the sort of man to inspire a response in a woman. He was just too...bland—and it didn't help that he was sitting next to Luke, who was anything but bland.

"...then there was the eighteenth hole," Jeremy was saying. "Father always uses a three wood on the eighteenth hole, but today my caddy handed me the driver.

Naturally I ended up in the water." He shook his head, his narrow lips turned into a frown. "He won't caddy for me again. I simply can't cope with that kind of mistake. It was a clear case of inattention."

"Inattention." Vicky's gaze fastened on Luke's hand curving around his glass. One nail was broken in the corner. Jeremy didn't have any broken nails—probably, Vicky suspected, because he had them manicured once a week. Luke had better things to do than get his nails manicured.

"It does make me wonder where they are getting these people," Jeremy went on. He looked at Luke. "Perhaps I should speak to them about engaging your services. It could be worth investigating."

Luke's lips twitched. "I, uh, don't do much of that anymore," he said very seriously. "But you can tell them to contact my partner, Barney. I'm sure he'd be glad to help out." His gaze met Vicky's, his eyes sparkling with laughter, and she had to bite down on her lip to hold in a giggle at the thought of the dour-looking Barney wandering around the golf course in his black suit.

Then he looked away, drained his glass and set it on the table. "Listen, I hate to cut this short but I'm going to have to leave."

"You are?" Jeremy's forehead furrowed. "I understood you were going to join me for dinner."

"I'm afraid I can't." Luke looked appropriately disappointed, while Vicky breathed a sigh of relief and started to rise. "I've got another engagement."

Jeremy swung his head to look at Vicky. "You don't have to leave, do you?"

Vicky searched for a way out. "Well, uh, Luke did drive me here and—"

"That's not a problem. I can take you home." Jeremy stretched across the table to cover her hand with his own pale one. "And it would give us time to get to know each other a little better."

Vicky swallowed. Getting to know Jeremy wasn't on the top of her list right now, but it should be. He was, after all, a good candidate for matrimony. Besides, maybe if Luke wasn't there to distract her, Jeremy might seem more...alive. "I'd like that," she lied. "If you're sure you wouldn't mind."

"Not at all," said Jeremy.

"Great." Luke shook hands with Jeremy. "Great to see you again. Good night, Vicky. You two enjoy yourselves." He beamed at them like a benevolent parent, then turned and wandered out.

Vicky watched him disappear. Maybe she should get to know Jeremy better, but she couldn't help wishing it was Luke she was going to get to know better instead.

7

"I CAN'T TELL YOU how much we appreciate you helping us find Pumffy," Suzette Harris oozed into Luke's ear. "Suzy hasn't been herself since he left."

"Neither has Barney," Luke mumbled. He shoved his hands in his pockets and watched his partner stroll around the room with the red-haired, wide-eyed Suzy clinging to his arm. Barney was wearing a tux. Suzy was wearing a vivid blue scrap of material that appeared to have been super-glued to her body. And together they looked exactly like a thug and his moll. Luke would have found it amusing if it hadn't been for the dazed expression on his partner's usually mournful face. As for Suzy, well, she did look a trifle anxious, although Luke suspected that was mostly because her "I've lost my doggy" trick hadn't forced Daddy to cough up any European vacation plans.

"Barney has been a tower of strength," Suzette confided. "I don't know what we would have done without him." She glanced at the couple and a small frown marred her extremely expensive face-lifted expression. "I hope he manages to find Pumffy soon."

"So do I," Luke agreed. The sooner Barney was away from Suzy, the better they all would be.

Suzette's frown increased in intensity. "I'd better just go check on her. She looks...upset. If you'll excuse me, Luke."

Luke watched her hurry to her daughter's side. Suzy didn't look so upset to him, but Suzette sure did. Suzy might get her trip to Europe, after all—not because of the dog, but because of Barney. Luke winced at that. Suzy in Europe wouldn't be a bad thing. He just hoped she'd go before Barney got too attached to her.

He watched them for a second, then checked the time. Ten o'clock. Jeremy and Vicky had been alone together for over two hours—assuming Vicky had stuck it out for that long. She hadn't looked impressed when he'd left.

Still, she had stayed with the guy—and why shouldn't she? Jeremy was everything she'd said she'd wanted in a man. It wasn't everything she should have, though. He tried to tell himself that Vicky was just a shallow socialite, but it didn't work. That lab didn't belong to a socialite—and neither did that apartment.

Barney materialized beside his elbow, his face drawn into a furtive expression. "Well?" he whispered. "Have you spotted anything suspicious yet?"

"Nope." Luke remembered the reason for his presence and scanned the room. There was nothing to see except a crowd of fashionably dressed men and women of various ages and descriptions sipping wine and eating hors d'oeuvres. None of them looked like dognappers to him. "Have you?"

"Just you," Barney grumbled. "You stand out like a sore thumb. Every time I look at you, you're glaring at these people as if you're going to shoot the lot of them. I wish you'd cut it out. You're making Suzy nervous."

Luke eyed the woman in question. She was talking to her mother, but she was watching Barney. "Suzy's making me nervous. She's a socialite, Barney. You don't want to get mixed up—"

"I'm not mixed up. I'm just looking for a dog." He peered at the crowd as if he expected Pumffy to appear at any moment. "What's got you so grumpy, anyway? Didn't Vicky and Jeremy hit it off?"

"They were doing fine when I left." By now they could be engaged. Now there was a really depressing thought.

"Terrific." Barney produced a wolfish grin, showing all his teeth. "With any luck they'll spend the night together and tomorrow our brief stint as a dating service will be over."

"Spend the night together?" Luke thought about Jeremy's carefully groomed hands touching Vicky and felt beads of sweat break out on his brow. "They're not going to spend the night together. Vicky isn't the type to sleep with someone on a first date."

"She isn't?" Barney's line of eyebrow came down. "I thought you said she was cold-blooded and conniving and only interested in snagging a rich husband."

"I did say that, but—"

"Well, if she wants to trap a husband, she might just think hopping into bed with him on the first date is the way to do it."

Luke got even colder. "Vicky isn't like that! She's an old-fashioned sort of woman. You should see her apartment. She's got antiques everywhere…along with about two thousand plants."

"Plants aren't good chaperons. Neither are antiques."

"Vicky doesn't need a chaperon." But Jeremy might. Luke passed a hand over his face. Vicky might not be the type to jump into bed on a first date, but what about Jeremy? True, he didn't look like he had a horny bone in his body, but looks could be deceiving—and Luke knew next to nothing about Jeremy's sexual preferences. Maybe he was the type to attack a woman on a first date.

Maybe he wouldn't even have to attack Vicky. From the sound of things, she didn't know much about dating! She didn't even know what golf clothes looked like! From the way she talked, it sounded as if her experience with men was limited to a few dates with sixty-year-old intellects who were more interested in her plants than her body. Jeremy wasn't a sixty-year-old university professor.

Perhaps leaving Jeremy to take Vicky home hadn't been a good idea. Or maybe he should have had a little talk with Vicky before he left her—made it clear that it was best to get to know someone before she got naked with them. But that would take time, and Vicky wasn't interested in giving things time. She wanted this over and done with, so she could concentrate on her work.

Now he really panicked.

"...AND THE HIGHLIGHT of the year was the third-quarter results," Jeremy explained earnestly. "We showed a financial gain of eighteen percent, which, when rolled forward..."

Vicky drained her wineglass and shook her head at the attentive waiter before he could refill it. She'd had more than enough wine. On the other hand, it was helping her get through an evening with Jeremy.

She had wanted to get to know him better. Well, she'd certainly done that. After a few hours in his company, she'd discovered quite a few things about him. He had a good background. He had a respectable career. He had outstandingly clean hands. And he would be a good remedy for insomnia.

Vicky seldom suffered from insomnia.

"Naturally Father and I were delighted," Jeremy intoned, his expression showing nothing close to delight. "So were the shareholders. I don't think there's any doubt about who will be taking over the company after Father retires."

"Oh?" Vicky tried to summon up an interest in Jeremy's life. "And when will that be?"

"Ten or fifteen years from now."

Great. If she married him, she'd have ten years of listening to him trying to make a big impression on Daddy and the stockholders so he could take over the business. Vicky closed her eyes. Maybe it wouldn't be too bad. He'd be involved in his career and she'd be involved with hers. They wouldn't have to spend that much time together.

And if she had trouble sleeping she'd know just what to do.

Jeremy patted a corner of his mouth with his napkin and made a surprising change of conversation. "So tell me, Victoria, what made you decide to leave Boston for Miami?"

Vicky briefly explained about the position at Oceanside. "I didn't want to leave, but Oceanside does have the best research facilities in North America."

"Oceanside? Ah, yes, the marine vegetation station." Jeremy pursed his lips. "You don't actually...work there, do you?"

"Yes, I do." His lips pursed further. Thin lips, Vicky noted. Not particularly kissable. "My research—"

"Research?" Jeremy raised a polite, inquiring eyebrow. "What sort of research would that be? Is it mainly library work, or do you actually get in the lab with all those...chemicals?"

Vicky blinked. "We try to use natural fertilizer whenever possible but there are—"

"It sounds a little...unusual." Jeremy knitted his brows. "But I suppose it does give you a little something to do now." He patted her hand. "Of course, after you're married, you'll have other things to occupy your time."

"My time is quite occupied now." Vicky eyed him through her lashes. "What other things?"

"For one thing, there's the social issue. Father says that married couples have a number of social obligations. It's the responsibility of the wife to handle those."

Yuck! Vicky cleared her throat. "I've never been one for those types of occasions." Jeremy looked alarmed and she smiled reassurance. "But I'm sure I could manage a few small dinner parties..." She could as long as there were caterers and florists and people like Gina in the world. And her mother. Her mother could come to visit...

"And then there are the children," Jeremy droned on. "Just finding a school for them can be a full-time job. Although in my case, it won't be difficult. I attended Swiltons. That's where my children will go."

"Swiltons?" Vicky vaguely recalled the name. "That's in Miami? I always thought it was in New York."

Jeremy nodded. "It is."

"But New York is a long way from Miami!"

Jeremy smiled indulgently. "It is a boarding school, Victoria. Father believed that children should be raised by professionals."

"I don't," Vicky muttered. She hadn't given much thought to how she'd manage a husband, a career and children, but she'd never considered sending infants away for months on end. Talk about a sterile environment!

"I mustn't forget the GlenMeadows Social Club," Jeremy continued. "Mother has been on the board for years. She spends months organizing social events, tournaments...the usual kind of thing. Naturally, my wife would work with her on that."

Vicky shifted in her chair. "I'm not very good at organizing—"

"Then there's the decorating. Mother goes through a new decorator every year. She says it keeps the house from going out of style."

"House?" Vicky said faintly.

"Yes." Jeremy oozed satisfaction. "My parents have a lovely house in Westhills. It's my intention to purchase one there myself."

"Westhills?" Westhills was miles from Oceanside. Not that it mattered. If she married Jeremy, she wouldn't have time to work. She'd be too busy finding a boarding school for her babies, socializing with the GlenMeadows Social Club, redecorating and generally turning into a clone of his mother.

She watched Jeremy chew a piece of steak. She couldn't do it. She couldn't spend the rest of her life with this guy. The only thing he had going for him was his ancestors and she was willing to bet that they wouldn't marry him, either.

Jeremy looked up from his meal. "Is something wrong, Victoria?"

"Not at all." Vicky picked up her fork. There was no graceful way out of this. She was going to have to spend at least another hour with Jeremy before she could get rid of him. Then she was going to call up Luke, no matter what time it was or who he was with, and give him a piece of her mind. This was all his fault. He'd set her up with this jerk. Why had he done that? Did he think she deserved a jerk like Jeremy? Or hadn't he realized Jeremy was a jerk? No, that was impossible. Luke was a detective. Surely they taught courses in jerk-recognition at detective school.

To be perfectly fair, though, she hadn't specified that she didn't want to marry a bland jerk with little personality and no original ideas. She'd just said she wanted someone with a good background and a respectable career. Gina had said that wasn't enough, and maybe Gina was right.

Maybe there were qualities in a husband that were just as important as their heritage.

VICKY WAS IN THE PROCESS of putting on a pot of coffee, and congratulating herself for surviving the evening, when someone knocked at her door. A check through the peephole showed Luke standing on the other side. He was still wearing his suit, which meant he hadn't stopped to change. His date mustn't have worked out, either. Good. It served him right for setting her up with Jeremy.

"Luke?" she said as she opened the door.

"Hi, Vicky." He peered over her shoulder. "I was, uh, in the neighborhood and thought I'd drop by to see how things went tonight with Jeremy."

He'd taken off his tie and unbuttoned the neck of his shirt. He looked so gorgeous that Vicky almost forgot her annoyance with him. "Who?"

"Jeremy." Luke peered over her shoulder, into the living room. "Is he still here?"

Right. Jeremy. The bozo he'd set her up with. "Oh, him," said Vicky. She turned on a heel and stomped into the kitchen. "No. He's gone, thank goodness."

"Thank goodness?" Luke trailed after her. "What happened? Didn't you two hit it off?"

"No." Vicky opened a cupboard. "Would you like some coffee?"

"Sure." He slouched against the doorway, his hands in his pockets and watched her pull two china mugs out of the cupboard. "What happened with Jeremy? I thought he was exactly what you wanted. And he seemed interested when I left."

"He was interested." Vicky poured coffee into the mugs. "At least, he was interested right up to the point where I said I was going to be spending the next three months in South America studying the grazing habits of the Pohepski sea horses." She carried the mugs over to the table and sat down. "That seemed to turn him right off."

Luke blinked astonishment. "You're going to South America?"

"Of course not! Even if I were, I wouldn't be studying Pohepski sea horses. There are no such things—and even if there were they wouldn't be grazing!" She smiled triumphantly as she recalled Jeremy's blank look when she'd made this announcement. "But Jeremy doesn't know that!"

His eyes widened farther. "You mean you *lied* to him!"

Did he think she was too old-fashioned to lie? "I certainly did." Then she felt compelled to add, "And it's completely out of character for me to do something like that. I'm usually a very honest person." She'd stopped being honest after she met him. "It probably comes from hanging around with detectives who do undercover surveillance."

"Just because I'm a detective doesn't mean I'm a compulsive liar." Luke leaned closer and peered into her eyes. "What happened tonight, anyway? Jeremy didn't try to get you drunk, did he?"

"No," said Vicky. "At least, not on purpose, although the only way anyone could get through an evening with Jeremy is if they've had a few drinks." She took a grateful sip of strong, dark coffee and glared at Luke over the cup. "Why in the world did you set me up with him?"

Luke blinked. "It wasn't my idea. You wanted to meet him."

"That's only because you said he was perfect."

"I didn't say he was perfect. I said he met all your qualifications and he does." Luke stretched back in his chair, his hands wrapped around his coffee. "He's from a good family. He's got a respectable career. And his fingernails—"

"Don't even mention his fingernails," Vicky warned. "That man has the most perfectly groomed hands I've ever seen."

Luke drew in a breath. "You said you wanted clean—"

"There is a difference between being clean and being overly clean. Jeremy is too clean."

Luke looked mildly astonished. "It's possible to be too clean?"

"Yes, and Jeremy is." Vicky thought of Jeremy and shuddered. "He's also got some outdated ideas about what women should and shouldn't do—and none of them have anything to do with sea vegetation! He thinks we should all take up golf and...and organize country club social events!"

"You don't like doing stuff like that?" Luke guessed.

"I don't know *how* to do stuff like that! I've never been able to understand why people golf and I can't organize anything. I don't even know how to order a pencil from office supplies!"

Luke's eyes sparkled with mirth. "I guess you'd be pretty much a wipeout at organizing a country club event."

"I certainly would. Besides, if I was doing that, when would I work? That's the whole point of finding a man in Miami—so I can stay at Oceanside." She shook her head. "I couldn't do that with Jeremy."

"That's a definite disadvantage," Luke agreed.

"Yes, it is. And besides all that, Jeremy also wants to send our children to a boarding school. People shouldn't send their own children away for someone else to raise! They should do it themselves...and they should *want* to do it themselves."

"That's true, but—"

"Jeremy might have the right background and clean fingernails, but that's the only thing he's got going for him. He's a dull, insipid man with an ego the size of Massachusetts. He can't talk about anything but his career. He even grooms his eyebrows, and he doesn't have anything that remotely resembles a sense of humor."

Luke's lip curled up into a half smile. "You did get to know him, didn't you?"

"Yes, I did. I... " Vicky narrowed her eyes. "You knew he was like that!"

Luke had the decency to look a little sheepish. "That is my opinion of him, but—"

"But you introduced me to him, anyway?" Vicky's voice rose. "If you knew he was like that, why would you recommend him to me?"

Luke winced. "He had all the other things you were looking for. And you never mentioned a sense of humor. How was I supposed to know it was important?"

He had a good point, but Vicky still held him squarely to blame. "Surely you could have guessed that, Luke! No one wants to marry a man who can't have a little fun now and then! Jeremy's idea of fun is to golf and he only does that because he thinks it's good for his career." She folded her arms. "Would you marry someone like that?"

Luke chuckled. "Well, no, but—"

"Neither would I," Vicky agreed. "And I'm not going to, either. You're simply going to have to find someone else."

"Someone else?" Luke repeated.

"That's right. Only this time, I want someone with a sense of humor. And he has to be more supportive of my career."

"Right," said Luke. "A good background. A respectable career. Clean, but not too clean, fingernails. A sense of humor and supportive. Is that all?"

"Probably not," said Vicky. "But it's a good start."

"Okay." He smiled his crinkly-eyed smile at her. "I'll start working on it first thing in the morning."

8

"SOMETIMES YOU PEOPLE just astonish me," Gina complained a couple of weeks later.

She crawled backward from underneath Vicky's desk and rose to her feet, brushing the dust off her cherry red walking shorts. "How did you manage to get a Ph.D. without learning how to wire up a computer?"

Vicky flipped a switch and sighed with relief as the screen came to life. "It wasn't easy. They kept trying to sneak in courses about it during biological isomorphism but we wouldn't have a thing to do with it!"

She brought up a graph of her latest statistics and began making adjustments. "Besides, that's why we need people like you around. They handle things we don't know how to handle." That reminded her of Luke. She'd hired him to handle something she didn't want to handle. Thank goodness she had, because it turned out that finding Mr. Right wasn't an easy task. She'd never have been able to do it herself.

She concentrated on her numbers. "Thanks for fixing this, Gina. I really need to get this done. Oh, and when I'm finished I'm going to scoot down to the lab for a while. Luke's supposed to drop by this afternoon, so if you see him, could you send him down there?"

"Luke?" Gina pounced on that. "Luke's coming here *again*?"

"Uh-huh."

"Don't tell me he's got another man lined up for you?"

"I think so." Vicky pressed a button and studied the resulting graph. Either she'd made a mistake, or those healthy carrots she'd just seen in the lab didn't exist.

"Not another one!" Gina gave her a disgusted look. "Haven't you realized yet that this isn't going to work?"

"It *is* going to work." Vicky corrected a mistake in her numbers and rechecked the graph. That was much better. There was a definite trend... "Although I must admit it's turning out to be a lot more difficult than I expected. It's no wonder I couldn't find anyone. Luke is having problems finding someone, and he's a professional."

"That's because you don't want him to find someone," Gina muttered.

Vicky stopped typing to look up at her. "What do you mean? Of course I want him to find somebody."

"I'm not so sure." Gina twirled a long strand of blond hair around a finger. "Luke's introduced you to a lot of men. If all you wanted was someone your parents would have approved of, you would be married with kids by now."

Vicky squirmed. Gina did have a point. Luke had found a number of qualified men for her. Since Jeremy there had been Leonard, Vincent, Marcus, Jonathan and Edwin. They were all close to okay, but there had always been a little something wrong with them. "I just want him to find someone who's...right. All the ones he's found so far have had something wrong with them." She thought about her most recent encounter.

"Take Edwin Thordyke, for example. He seemed like a good one. He's a direct descendant of one of the Philadelphia Thordykes. He's got a degree in history, and another one in law. My father would have liked him, and so would my mother."

"But you didn't?" Gina guessed.

Vicky made a face. "No. Don't date a history professor, Gina. All they talk about is history—at least, that's all Edwin talked about. He spent two hours going on and on about his ancestors and my ancestors. I think he knows more about them than they knew about themselves."

"That's a bad thing?"

"It's not a good thing. He was more interested in my long-deceased relatives than he was in me."

Gina cleared her throat. "I thought you were interested in their ancestors, too."

Vicky shrugged. "I want them to have good ancestors, of course. But it would be nice if they'd show a little interest in me personally. We are talking about spending the rest of our lives together. Don't you think we should have some interest in each other?"

Gina blinked. "Yes, but...but I didn't think you agreed."

Vicky gave her a derisive look. "Naturally, I agree. I don't want a man who only cares about my Uncle Willie whom I never see, or my great-great grandparents whom I've never met."

"I can understand that." Gina waited for a heartbeat. "What about Luke? He doesn't seem interested in your uncle or your long-deceased relations."

"He isn't." Vicky kept typing from her list. "Luke

doesn't care about stuff like that. He's just interested in finding lost kids and putting families back together."

"And you," Gina purred. "He's also interested in you."

Vicky gave a little laugh, flustered by the notion. "Don't be silly, Gina. Luke is just doing a job, that's all. He's not interested in me."

"Luke isn't interested in you?" Gina snorted. "How can someone with numerous degrees be so dumb? He's always hanging around here, Vicky. I see more of him than I do of Dr. Franklin and *he* never goes home."

She was right. Luke did spend a great deal of his time here, and at her apartment. He often dropped by, armed with a bag of take-out food, to tell her about another man he'd found, or one he was considering investigating. "He has to spend some time with me, Gina. I hired him—"

"To do what? Investigate sea vegetables?" Gina shook her head. "I don't think so. And it's not because you're his client, either. If he spent this much time with all his clients, then all he'd have time to do is *visit* clients. He'd never solve any cases."

"He's just...thorough."

"Nonsense. He's got the hots for you, Vicky, and you feel the same way."

"I do *not*," Vicky insisted. "Oh, I admit I like Luke. Who wouldn't like him? He's a nice person. But that's all there is to it. I know very well that Luke is not the right man for me." She paused. "And I'm sure I'm not Luke's type, either."

"FIND A HUSBAND for Vicky and a dognapper for Barney," Luke muttered to himself. "Who says I don't get the interesting cases?"

He stopped in front of a store window and watched the action on the street in the reflection. There wasn't much of it. The shimmering heat of the sun bouncing off the sidewalk pavement. A few scantily dressed people wandering down the street...and a benign-looking man wearing denim shorts and a white T-shirt lugging a sack of dog food through the parking area of a strip mall.

Luke watched as his quarry stopped beside a red minivan and heaved his load inside. This fellow wouldn't do for either case. There was no way he was a dognapper, and he wouldn't do as a husband for Vicky. Three little girls calling him Daddy suggested he'd already filled that position for someone else. Besides, Luke doubted Vicky would want three little girls.

Luke, on the other hand, would love a carful of kids.

He waited until the minivan pulled away, then pushed his hands into his pockets and strolled back the way he'd come. Someday he'd meet the right woman, and he'd be the one heaving sacks of dog food into a minivan filled with children. He scratched the dog food out of the picture. After this canine episode with Barney he wasn't positive he'd ever want to own a pet.

He stopped beside Barney's black sedan parked across the street from the strip mall. "Next time we go out together can we take my car?" he asked as he climbed inside. "A black sedan isn't a good stakeout vehicle. It looks like, at any minute, gangsters are going to jump out of it with machine guns." He took in his partner's black-suited, long-faced figure. "And it doesn't help that you're a dead ringer for Al Capone."

Barney gave him a disgusted look from under his heavy dark eyebrows. "Will you please forget the jokes and tell me what you found out."

"Nothing." Luke rested his head back against the headrest and closed his eyes. "There was nothing to find out. There's no way that guy has anything to do with dognapping."

Barney's tone still hinted at suspicion. "Are you sure?"

"I'm positive. I tailed him to his car. It was a minivan, Barn. Sophisticated, dognapping criminals don't drive minivans."

"You can't be sure—"

"Besides, there were three little girls sitting in the back. They all called him Daddy."

"That doesn't mean—"

"There were three little Welsh terriers back there with them."

"Oh," said Barney. "Well, I suppose that could explain why he bought so much dog food."

"It could," Luke agreed. "However it doesn't explain why I was following him in the first place." He shifted sideways to face Barney. "There wasn't anything suspicious about him. All he did was buy a bag of doggy biscuits."

Barney gave him a look of disdain. "It wasn't just any doggy biscuits, Luke. It was Rothwell and Lewis Canine Excellence Dog Chow for Select Breeds. Not only is that stuff expensive, but it's also the only thing that Pumffy will eat. And according to the store owner, that guy buys it once a week."

Luke groaned and dropped his head into his hand. "Why me?" he asked the world. "I'm a good person. Do I really deserve a partner who has lost all touch with reality?"

Barney scowled. "I haven't lost touch with reality. I'm just looking for Pumffy."

Luke peered at him through his fingers. "That's exactly what I mean. You've been looking for that dog for weeks now, and you still haven't gotten one solid lead! When are you going to give up on this?"

Barney tapped his fingers against the steering wheel while he considered it. "About the same time you give up on finding Vicky a husband," he finally concluded.

Luke stared at him in amazement. "Why should I give up on that?"

"Because you don't want to find her a husband?"

"I do so!"

"Then why haven't you done it yet? This was only supposed to take a couple of days." Barney checked his watch. "We're at the three-week mark now."

Luke leaned back against the brown upholstery and folded his arms. "That's not my fault. I've introduced her to at least half a dozen men—and that doesn't include the half dozen she rejected without meeting them. I can't help it if she changed from unpicky to superpicky."

"It's Vicky's fault, is it?"

"Yes," Luke insisted. "She keeps changing her mind about what she wants. At first, all she wanted was a man with a decent background, a solid career and clean fingernails. Now her list could cover three pages." Luke began listing them off on his fingers. "He has to have a sense of humor, be supportive of her work, be the right age—not too old and not too young. He has to like kids, but not want them right away, and he can't have ever mentioned the words *boarding school*. He can't have political ambitions and he has to have a social conscience, whatever that means."

"Whatever it means, I'd say you've got it." Barney paused. "Along with all the other requirements."

Luke shook his head. "I don't. I'm a private detective from North Dakota, not a stockbroker or shipping magnate with a bunch of ancestors who landed here five seconds after the dinosaurs left. That's what Vicky wants."

"That's what she says she wants." Barney raised his long face and looked wise. "It's not what she really wants. She's just not very clever, Luke. Not like Suzy."

Luke groaned out loud. He'd heard enough about Suzy's virtues to last a lifetime. "Not Suzy again. Is it possible for us to have just one conversation without her name being mentioned?"

Barney folded his arms and compressed his lips. "What's that supposed to mean?"

"Just that every time you open your mouth these days, Suzy's name seems to pop out."

Barney shrugged. "She's a fascinating person. Just the other day she was telling me about the course she took in Mediterranean Mediation Techniques. It's interesting stuff."

"Suzy took a course in Mediterranean Mediation Techniques, did she?" Luke looked over at his partner. "Tell me something, Barn. Is there anything Suzy hasn't taken a course in?"

"Not much." Barney took on the now-familiar hit-by-a-bus expression he got every time Suzy's name was mentioned. "She's got a lot of interests."

"Sure, she does," Luke said skeptically. Suzy sounded like a lot of other rich kids he'd run into. They drifted around, filling in their time by taking one course after another, never really accomplishing anything, with their one goal in life to acquire possessions.

"She does," Barney insisted. "She's a smart woman, Luke."

"I'll tell you what smart is. Vicky is smart. She's got a Ph.D. You should see the setup she's got down at her lab. She—"

"She might know a lot about plants, but she sucks when it comes to knowing herself. Sort of like you."

Luke frowned at that. "What are you talking about? I know lots about myself."

"No, you don't! And you can't convince me you're trying to find her a husband. I've met some of those dweebs you've set her up with—and I wouldn't marry them, either."

Luke chuckled and slouched lower. "I don't see them proposing to you, Barn."

"Up yours," Barney said politely. "The point is, you're not finding men that little Ms. Vicky would even consider marrying."

Luke shifted uneasily. "I'm giving it my best shot."

"No, you aren't. If I can look at those guys and know they're jerks, then you can do the same thing. You know darn well she won't like them. And the reason you're doing that is because *you* are interested in the woman yourself."

"That's not how it is." But Luke had an uneasy feeling that Barney wasn't far off the mark. Oh, there was nothing blatantly wrong with the men he was finding for Vicky, but he was never surprised at the things she didn't like about them. They were usually exactly the same things he didn't like about them. That was just a coincidence, though. "She's not my type."

"But you are attracted to her."

Luke thought about Vicky, perched on a lab stool, her forehead furrowed into endearing lines as she earnestly explained sea vegetation to him. "I suppose I'm nominally attracted to her, but—"

"Nominally?"

Luke shrugged helplessly. "Okay, maybe a little more than nominally. But that doesn't mean anything. Vicky's busy looking for the right man, and it's not me. I'm looking for the right woman, and that's not her. She's a socialite. Maybe a little different from the usual brand of socialite but she still is one. I don't want a woman like that."

"Sure, you don't." Barney gestured toward the store. "Hey, there's another guy with that dog food. Are you going to follow him, or am I?"

"I'm NOT SURE there's any point in even meeting Reginald," Vicky decided that afternoon.

She sat sideways on a lab stool, crossed her legs and handed Luke the three closely typed pages containing everything there was to know about Reginald. "I don't think he's the right type."

"He isn't?" Luke reread the information, then looked back up at her. "He sounds like the right type. He's got his own architecture firm, his family has a strong Boston connection, he's clean, he tells great jokes, he does a lot of fund-raising for the inner-city kids...and I swear to God he's got more personality than Jeremy."

"That wouldn't be difficult," Vicky muttered.

Luke winced and held up a hand. "I know Jeremy was a mistake but Reg isn't. There isn't a thing wrong with him."

"Maybe there isn't, but...well, he just doesn't sound very interesting. And he doesn't look interesting, either."

"He doesn't?" Luke peered at the photograph. "He's not a bad-looking guy—if you like the clean-cut blond type, that is." He grinned. "Personally I think the disheveled detective types are a lot better, but it's a matter of opinion."

It was an opinion Vicky shared. She watched Luke lean back, with one elbow propped against the lab counter. He was wearing his usual outfit of casual brown pants, a T-shirt and a brown tweed jacket with leather on the elbows. He looked as relaxed and at home in her lab as he had at Madalyne's party. No wonder he was a good detective. He seemed to have the ability to blend in with his surroundings as if he belonged there. He sure looked as if he belonged in her lab.

Luke waved a hand in front of her face. "Earth to Vicky. Earth to Vicky. Is there anyone in there?"

"Sorry." Vicky gave her head a shake. "My mind was wandering. That, uh, happens to me a lot when I'm in here." Actually, it happened a lot when Luke was in here. She swallowed. "What were we talking about?"

Luke swiveled on the stool and his knees bumped

against hers. "Reginald. You were telling me what was wrong with him."

"Oh, yes." His knees felt good pressed against hers. Far too good as a matter of fact. Vicky slid off the stool and picked up her clipboard. "Well, uh, it says there that he's interested in politics. That won't do."

"He's not that interested in them! He just does a little work for a political party every so often." Luke shoved a hand through his already rumpled hair. "Besides, what's wrong with politics? Your Uncle Willie—"

"Just because Uncle Willie is a politician doesn't mean my family approves of politicians." Vicky wandered over to check the temperature reading on one of the four growing chambers in an attempt to stop herself from noticing how cute Luke looked with his hair messed up. "Besides, if he wants to go into politics he'll expect his wife to do a bunch of...political stuff. I can't do that. It would interfere with my work."

Luke groaned and dropped his forehead into a palm. "Oh no. Not another qualification! What does that make it? Thirty-three things now? Or is it thirty-four?"

"I'm sure it's only five or six," Vicky objected.

"No, it isn't. This list is getting longer than my arm." He read from it. "Good family. Respectable career. Clean fingernails. Sense of humor. Not too tall. Not too short. Not too old. Not too young. Not too obsessed with his appearance, although he has to be a good dresser, not a crook, have a social conscience, be interested in the environment...now no political aspirations."

Vicky raised her chin. "They're not outrageous requirements. I have to spend the rest of my life with this guy. I don't want to make a mistake." In truth, she was a little surprised at how picky she was getting. It seemed that every time she met a man, she discovered something else she needed in one.

"They might not be outrageous requirements but they're not easy requirements, either," Luke complained. "Do you have any idea how hard it is to find a man like this?"

"Yes." She looked over at him, concerned. "I tried myself and I didn't have any luck, but...well, you can do it, can't you?"

Luke's eyes met hers, and he smiled his crinkly-eyed smile. "Anything for you." For a second Vicky thought that maybe Gina was right, that maybe he was interested. Then he looked away. "Of course it might take me the rest of my natural life to do it."

Vicky felt a pang of guilt. "I didn't realize this was going to be difficult for a detective when I asked you to do it."

"Neither did I," Luke grumbled.

"And I didn't think it would take so much time, either." She faced him. "I'm sure you've got other things to do that are more important than finding me a husband."

Luke shrugged. "All my clients are important."

"But you're spending so much time on this. You always seem to be here..."

"Just part of my job," Luke said easily. "I have to spend time with you so I can find out more about you—and about the type of man you like." He grinned. "Besides, I like to keep track of your progress on this sea carrot thing. I'm seriously concerned that if you don't make some headway with it, I might be stuck eating one-inch-long vegetables someday."

So much for Gina's theory that he was interested in her! "You don't need to worry about that. My experiments are showing a lot of promise. I should be able to keep you in healthy vegetables for the rest of your days."

"That's a load off my mind." Luke checked his watch. "I'd better get going. I've got to scour the city for another man for you and help Barney track down a dog."

Vicky gave him a questioning look. "Barney wants a dog?"

"Unfortunately, yes." Luke scrubbed a fist along his jaw. "I'm really starting to wonder about him. He's got me doing the weirdest things."

"You don't have to do it, do you? Couldn't you say no?"

"To Barney?" Luke shook his head. "I can't say no to Barney. He looks at me with that mournful face and I feel guilty as sin. Besides, I owe him."

"You do?" Vicky kept watching him. "Why?"

"He helped me out a while ago. I made a dumb mistake and Barney was right there."

"What happened?" Vicky eyed his healthy-looking body. "You didn't get shot, did you?"

Luke chuckled. "No, nothing like that. I just got involved with the wrong type of woman."

Now Vicky was really curious. "What was wrong with her?"

"Not a whole lot, I suppose." He sighed. "She just wasn't as interested in me as she was in Edgar Snow's pocket book."

Someone had dumped him for a walletful of cash? "She mustn't have been very bright, then."

Luke's lips turned into a wry half smile. "I don't think either of us were very bright. She shouldn't have gotten mixed up with me because she knew I wasn't her type, and I shouldn't have gotten mixed up with her because I knew she wasn't my type."

"Oh?" said Vicky, intrigued. "What exactly is your type?"

"Nice," Luke said immediately. "Down to earth. Pretty, but not the kind that worries about their appearance. Someone who cares a lot about stuff other people think is silly, like a nurse or a teacher." His brow furrowed. "And I want a family someday, so she has to want a family, and it has to be important to her. I've seen too many situations where both parents are so busy they don't have time for things like that." He paused reflectively. "And she can't have any social connections, either. I don't want someone who'd rather spend their life at the GlenMeadows Country Club, instead of doing something worthwhile."

Vicky frowned. "You don't want a woman, Luke. You want a saint."

"Not quite." He grinned lecherously. "She also has to look good in black stockings and really know how to fill out a bra."

Great. He wanted a sexy temptress with a heart of gold. Good thing he wasn't her Mr. Right because she certainly wasn't his Mrs. Right. "You're going to need a detective to find a woman like that."

"I *am* a detective, and so far I haven't had much luck." His got to his feet, his eyes twinkling with mischief. "Maybe I should turn the case over to Barney. It might help him forget about this dog thing. And who knows? Maybe he would find me the perfect mate." He wandered out the door, chuckling to himself.

Vicky watched him leave. "If Barney finds you the perfect woman, I will sink him in swamp water," she muttered after him.

That wasn't fair. Luke was trying to find her the perfect man. Why shouldn't he find the perfect woman?

She focused back on her readings, but she'd forgotten where she'd left off and had to start over. Darn Luke, anyway. And darn this stupid find-a-husband project. No matter what she did, it interfered with her work!

9

"I'VE MET LOTS of men, Mother," Vicky reported during an early-morning phone conversation with her mother. "Lots and lots of men." She took the portable phone with her into the kitchen, talking while she walked. "I just couldn't marry any of them."

"You couldn't?" Her mother sounded completely flummoxed by this. "Why not? What was wrong with them?"

I couldn't imagine myself sleeping with any of them. "They...weren't my type." Vicky flipped through a folder of potential candidates Luke had left for her to review. None of them had awakened any spark of interest in her. "It's not easy to find the right man here."

Her mother sighed sympathetically. "I suppose that's only to be expected, dear. After all, you do live in Miami. I'm sure it's more difficult to find someone there than it would be in a more civilized city, like Boston or Philadelphia."

"That's true." Or was it? She was beginning to wonder if the man she wanted existed on the planet.

"Perhaps you should consider coming back here," her mother suggested hesitantly. "Harold Wellington still isn't married. You do remember him, don't you?"

Vicky had a vague recollection of him. "He's got beady eyes, Mother. I couldn't marry someone like that. Think of the children."

"Victoria..."

"Besides, I can't work at Oceanside and live in Boston. The commute would be too much for me."

"I understand it would be difficult but—"

"It would be impossible," Vicky stated firmly. "Don't worry, Mother. I'm sure I'll find someone here soon."

She made a face as she hung up the phone. There she went again, telling another lie. Deceit was starting to be a way of life.

She wandered around her apartment, gathering up the papers and books she'd brought home with her last night. The truth was, she had serious doubts that she was ever going to meet someone that she wanted to marry. She'd met a number of men who would please her parents—nice men, kind men, men a lot of women would be happy to set up housekeeping with—but she had yet to meet a man she wanted to spend the rest of her life with.

She was starting to wonder if the problem was with the men, or if it was with her.

"Maybe you were right," she confessed to Gina during a rare coffee break that afternoon. "Maybe this isn't going to work."

"I hate to say I told you so, but I told you so." Gina slid gracefully into a chair and gave her skirt that downward pull. "You can't hire someone—"

"It's not the hiring part that's wrong," Vicky interrupted. "There's nothing wrong with hiring someone to find me a husband. It saved me a lot of time and I'm glad I did. It's the finding part. I'm just not sure there's a man out there to be found."

"Oh?" Gina digested that for a moment. "What

makes you think that? Did you have another date last night?"

Vicky nodded. "Yes. Luke introduced me to Alexander."

"Don't tell me. Let me guess. Alexander didn't work out, either."

"No."

"What was wrong with him? Was he too tall, too short, too stuffy, too grubby, too clean, too involved in illegal activities?"

"None of the above," Vicky reported. "He actually had quite a few good qualities. He was clean, pleasant, polite, and he had a great sense of humor. He even asked me about my work and said he thought it sounded fascinating." She said this with a sense of amazement. Most men's eyes glazed over when she told them what she did.

"Ah," said Gina. "Does that mean we're going to hear the symphony of wedding bells soon?"

Vicky shook her head. "Not mine, I'm afraid—at least, not with Alexander. I couldn't marry him, Gina. He's far too athletic!"

"Too athletic?" Gina raised a perfect eyebrow. "It's possible to be too athletic?"

"It certainly is! Alexander spent a good hour talking about tennis, football and hockey." Vicky wrinkled her nose. "After a while, that topic gets a little old. And besides talking about them, I think he does them all."

Gina didn't seem to see the importance of that. "So what? I'm sure your ancestors were sporty types. They'd have to be to chop wood and...and grow corn and build four-story mansions in the classier parts of North America."

"They didn't all build mansions," Vicky objected. "Only some of them built classy mansions. And I'm sure they didn't spend an entire evening flexing their muscles."

"Alexander did that?"

"Constantly." Vicky shuddered as she thought about it. "It's impossible to carry on a decent conversation with someone who is doing that. It's far too distracting."

Gina smirked. "Sounds like a distraction I could handle."

"Gina!"

Gina held up a hand. "Hey, there's nothing wrong with being attracted to a man! So he's not Mr. Intellectually Stimulating. If you're attracted to him..."

"Unfortunately, I wasn't attracted to Alexander." Vicky put a hand over her stomach in remembrance. "Watching those muscles go up and down and up and down came close to making me seasick. I don't want to spend the rest of my life married to a man who makes me nauseous when I look at him."

Gina giggled, then sobered. "Unfortunately?"

"Hmmm?"

"You said that unfortunately you weren't attracted to Alexander. Why is that unfortunate?"

Vicky started to say, "never mind," then reconsidered. She'd like to discuss this with somebody. Gina was a good friend, and she knew a lot more about the subject than Vicky did. "I was just hoping I would be." She sat back down in her chair and gave Gina a glum look. "I'm starting to think that there's something wrong with me."

Gina sat down beside her. "Like what?"

"I don't know. Maybe I've got some sort of hormone imbalance problem. I understand that when women reach a certain age—"

"You're thirty, Vicky, not fifty!" Gina frowned. "Why would you suggest that, anyway?"

"The way things are going." Vicky waved around a hand. "Look at the statistics. I've been out with more than half a dozen men this month and I haven't been attracted to any of them! Granted, they all had things wrong with them, but you'd think I'd feel a little...something." She shook her head. "But I didn't."

Gina drew her brows together. "You didn't?"

"Nope."

"Not a twinge? A tingle? A spark?"

Vicky shook her head.

"Oh." Gina nibbled delicately on the edge of a brilliant orange fingernail while she considered that. "Well, it's probably nothing to do with you and more to do with them," she finally concluded. "Maybe they just weren't attractive."

"Some of them were. Dwight was handsome. So was Ralston. And Alexander was tall, blond and muscular. But I just couldn't warm up to them." Vicky looked down at her hands. "Maybe I should see a doctor."

"And say what? I've met a whole bunch of men I'm not attracted to?" Gina shook her head. "That's not a medical condition, honey. It's a fact of life. And I'm sure there's nothing wrong with you. After all, you have been attracted to other men. Like Luke, for example. Aren't you attracted to him?"

Vicky thought about Luke's crinkly-eyed smile and shivered. "Yes, I'm attracted to Luke! I'd have to be comatose not to be. You've met him. He's good-looking and intelligent, and you should just see him in shorts! I could hardly keep my eyes on the ball when we were playing tennis."

Gina's eyebrows lifted. "*You* were playing tennis?"

"Uh-huh. Luke thought I should know something about the game before I met Alexander." She pictured Luke running around the tennis court with those great legs and great arms, with just the right amount of muscles, and got all shivery again. "But I wasn't attracted to Alexander and I am attracted to Luke, even though he's not who I'm supposed to be attracted to!" She folded her arms, and pouted her lips together. "It just doesn't make sense. If I can be attracted to a man who doesn't meet my qualifications, why can't I be attracted to one who does?"

Gina patted her shoulder. "You can't predict these things. Chemistry is chemistry."

"That's no help!" Vicky jumped to her feet and paced across the room. "Isn't there something I can do about it?"

"Well," Gina said thoughtfully. "You could always seduce him."

"Seduce who? Luke?" Vicky stopped walking. "I couldn't do that! Luke is all wrong for me. He's—"

"A cretin from North Dakota. I know. I know. But I didn't say marry him. I said seduce him." Gina waved a hand around, her eyes sparkling with mischief. "Cut loose. Have an affair, a fling."

Vicky scowled at her. "I'm a Sommerset-Hayes Gina. We don't do flings!"

"You don't?" Gina's eyes widened. "You mean you've never...flinged?"

"No." Vicky twisted her fingers together. "There

was Boswell, but he wasn't a fling. He was an architect."

"Boswell?" Gina snorted. "You dated a man named Boswell?"

"Yes, I did!" Gina giggled and Vicky elaborated. "He's related to Randolf Cramer, who happens to be from an extremely prominent Boston family."

"Oh," said Gina. "Well, then, uh, why didn't you marry him? It sounds like your parents would have approved."

Vicky nodded. "My parents did approve. They were the ones who set it up. And I would have married him, I guess, except the offer came from Oceanside and I accepted. That pretty much ended any chance of marrying him." She sighed. "It's one of the reasons my parents were so upset about the move."

"Oh," said Gina.

"And I didn't seduce him. I wouldn't have a clue how to go about doing something like that—even if I wanted to."

"It's easy." Gina gave a careless shrug. "You just invite him over for dinner and serve it wearing nothing but a pair of high heels and a black garter belt with stockings. Most men usually get the hint right away— although it can take until dessert to get through to a few of them."

Vicky pictured herself dishing up a microwave vegetarian entrée to Luke, dressed in the garments Gina had described. "He'd get the hint all right. He'd look for a woman who could cook."

"Trust me," Gina said archly. "Food would be the last thing on his mind."

"You're right. If I tried that on Luke he'd be so busy

laughing he'd forget he hadn't eaten. Either that, or he'd say something condescending like, 'Great garter belt, Vicky. It makes you look so old-fashioned.'"

Gina shook her head. "I don't think Luke—"

"Yes, he would," Vicky interrupted. "And he'd be right. The other day when I was shopping I tried on one of those string bikini things—you know the kind you see women wearing on the beach all the time. They look sexy and attractive and modern—like Cindy Crawford clones. I didn't look anything like Cindy Crawford. I looked more like Julie Andrews in a string bikini!"

"You went shopping?" Gina looked astonished. "You're really branching out, aren't you?"

Vicky ignored her. "It doesn't matter, anyway. Luke doesn't see me that way. And I don't see him that way, either."

"But you said..."

"I know I'm attracted to him, but that's all there is to it. Once I meet the right man, I'll stop feeling this way about Luke." She'd stop seeing him at all. That idea didn't delight her—but it would be for the best. Besides, after she'd found her husband, she'd be thinking about him. Then this itch for Luke would go away.

"I still think you should seduce him," said Gina.

"I don't," Vicky said firmly. "I don't want to seduce Luke." The heat in her body intensified. She bit on her bottom lip. "But maybe I should consider seducing someone else."

"His name is Spencer Lewiston, he's a stockbroker and his great-great-uncle had an affair with Paul Revere's wife," Luke reported a couple of evenings later. "How does he sound?"

"Immoral?" Vicky guessed. Immoral was how she was feeling. She was curled up in a corner of the sofa with a research book open in front of her. Luke was sprawled on the floor, with his back against her grandfather's dark green armchair, his papers spread all around him. He was wearing a pair of faded jeans and a brown shirt with the top buttons opened, and he looked casual and masculine and far too appealing.

Luke chuckled. "I was just kidding about that part. I doubt Paul Revere's wife had an affair. Spencer's great-great-uncle was related to someone involved in the Boston Massacre—on our side, of course. He plays squash twice a month, he doesn't have a lot of muscles, his teeth are his own and his favorite color is green."

"That's...fascinating." Vicky murmured. "But how does he feel about seduction?"

Luke glanced up, startled. "What?"

Way to go, Vicky. "I asked how he feels about rain forests," Vicky improvised. "I don't want someone who doesn't care about ecology."

Luke grinned, slow and lazy, and his eyes crinkled at the corners. "I knew that—and I've got some information about it somewhere." He riffled through the papers strewn around him while Vicky mentally riffled through her lingerie drawer. She didn't own a garter belt of any description. She did have an attractive set of pale green lingerie, but that wouldn't do. Pale green was definitely old-fashioned.

Luke found his paper. "Ah, here it is. Let's see. Spencer is strongly in favor of rain forests and strongly against logging."

"That's...good." Did *Spencer's* forehead furrow into sexy lines when he read from a page?

"Good?" Luke looked up, exasperated. "This isn't just good, Vicky. It's an outstanding piece of detective work! Do you know how hard it is to find out how someone feels about rain forests?"

"No. But I'm sure it's not easy." She smiled into his eyes. "And I really appreciate all the extra work you're doing."

Luke smiled back, his green eyes going soft and warm and dark before he cleared his throat and focused back on his papers. "No problem," he muttered from somewhere deep in his chest. "Anything to make you happy."

Then how about if he took off his clothes? Better yet, how about if he took off her clothes? She pictured Luke's long, tanned fingers on the buttons of her blouse and her palms started to sweat.

"How about it?" Luke asked. "Is Spencer a definite maybe or an outright rejection?"

Vicky shrugged. "I suppose I should meet him."

"Okay. He's going to be at the Daniels family open house Friday night. You can meet him there."

Vicky came back to earth with a start. "But I'm not going to the—"

Luke scowled. "Yes, you are. Spencer will definitely be there."

"But—"

"But nothing." He aimed a finger at her. "I've busted my buns getting this information for you. The least you can do is go to one little party. Besides, it's a good way for you to meet him."

"I suppose it is," said Vicky, trying not to think about his buns. "But isn't there some other way?"

"Not that I can think of." Luke rested an elbow on top of the couch. "I'm running out of innovative ways for you to meet these guys. You can darn well run into Spencer at the Daniels house." He picked up a page. "Besides, if I have to go, you should have to go."

"You're going to be there?"

"Uh-huh." He grinned. "Actually, I'm killing two birds with one stone. I'll be there to introduce you to Spencer, and I can also do some clandestine investigating, as well."

"Investigating of what?" Vicky asked.

Luke shrugged. "I can't say. Client-detective confidentiality and all that. Just keep an eye on the Daniels dog. I hear he's been acting suspicious lately."

"Sure," said Vicky. She watched him review the papers spread around the floor. "Luke?"

"Hmmm?"

"How do you go about seducing someone?"

Luke spluttered and spilled some of his soft drink all down his shirt. "How do I *what?*"

"Seduce someone."

"I don't...I..." He stopped to gape at her. "Why are you asking this?"

"I just wondered," said Vicky.

"Why were you wondering? You're not planning on seducing Spencer, are you?" He looked horrified. "I agree he sounds perfect, but you haven't even met him yet. Don't you think you should at least be introduced before you start planning a seduction scene?"

"I wasn't planning a seduction scene! I was just wondering how I'd do it if I was."

"So you decide to ask *me?*" He looked at her with interest. "What makes you think I know?"

Because you're the sexiest man I've ever met, and I don't ever notice sexy men. Women who notice that kind of thing would be all over you in two minutes. "Because you're a detective," said Vicky.

"Right." Luke nodded wisely. "And in the movies us detectives are always getting seduced." He sighed. "Unfortunately, that's not the way it works in real life. In the movies, those guys don't spend their lives chasing down runaway kids. You don't meet a whole lot of gorgeous women anxious to jump your bones doing that."

"You mean a woman has never..."

Luke's cheekbones reddened. "I didn't say that."

"Good," said Vicky. "Then you are a good person to ask."

"No, I'm not." Luke scrubbed a hand over his face and gave her an impatient look. "Why do you have to ask anyone? You must know something about this. I mean surely you've..."

Vicky shook her head.

"You mean you've never, uh—"

"Seduced someone?" Vicky shook her head again. "No. Seduction wasn't one of the courses offered...even in a public school."

Luke cleared his throat. "What about a...a girlfriend? Gina, for example. She must—"

"Gina's idea was to wear black stockings, a garter and nothing else." Vicky shook her head. "That's not me."

"I suppose not, although it's definitely me." He eyed her. "I think you'd need a more subtle approach. What about your mother? Didn't she impart any wisdom on the subject?"

Vicky pictured her short, round, immaculate mother and shook her head. "I doubt Mother knows anything more about seduction than I do."

"Figures," Luke muttered. He swallowed. "But you have, uh, have some experience with...men, haven't you?"

First Gina, then him! Did everyone think she'd been locked up in a lab all her life? "Of course I've had some experience! I'm thirty years old. There's no such thing as a thirty-year-old virgin anymore."

"Darn few at any rate," Luke agreed.

"But that was quite a while ago, and I didn't seduce him," Vicky admitted. "We discussed it and made a rational decision about it."

"A rational decision, huh?" Luke nodded approval. "That sounds very...mature. A little cut-and-dried, but mature."

"It was." It had been mature, but it had also been pretty cut-and-dried. "However, that was in Boston. Things are different in Miami."

Luke cleared his throat. "You mean you haven't...been with a man since you moved here?"

"No," said Vicky. "I don't sleep around. Besides, I'm not the sort of woman who inspires that kind of reaction in a man." She certainly hadn't in him. "It's probably my upbringing. I wasn't brought up to be sexy."

Luke looked puzzled. "You can bring up someone to be sexy?"

"You must be able to," said Vicky. "Look at Gina. She's sexy. Men are all over her. Even Dr. Fisher drools over her, and he doesn't notice anything that doesn't have fins. I don't inspire that kind of response in anyone. As a matter of fact, I doubt Dr. Fisher knows I'm female."

"Then Dr. Fisher isn't very observant," said Luke. "I noticed it right away." He winked. "Of course, I'm a detective. We're trained to notice things like that."

Did men have to be trained observers to realize what sex she was? "Thanks a lot," Vicky grumbled. "I guess that's something else I should add to my list. He's going to need a detective course so he can notice that I'm the opposite sex."

"Why not? Good background, great career, outstanding personality, clean hands, a zillion other qualities...plus a detective school background." He chuckled. "There's tons of men like that in Miami!"

Not tons. Just Luke. Vicky pursed her lips at the idea. Unfortunately he wasn't right for her, either.

Luke took a look at her expression and grew serious. "Hey, it's not that bad. I'm sure lots of men have noticed that you don't look like they do."

"I don't think so."

Luke made another attempt. "What about the ones I've set you up with? Haven't they tried—"

"No," said Vicky. She began listing them off. "Jeremy shook my hand. Milton kissed my cheek. Harlin tipped his hat. The only one who even tried to come into my apartment was Gerald, and that was just because he wanted to talk about my uncle. If Uncle Willie had been there, Gerald might have attacked him, but he wasn't interested in attacking me."

Luke bent his head and rubbed the back of his neck, hard. "I thought you didn't like any of them."

"I didn't. And I didn't want them to try to...to do

something I didn't want them to do." Vicky leaned forward. "But if I had wanted them to do something, how would they have known?"

Luke looked back at her, frowning. "You don't want them to do anything."

"But sooner or later I'm going to meet—"

"I don't care who you meet." Luke furrowed his brows and looked stern. "You're not going to seduce any of them. You shouldn't even be kissing them. You go around kissing a man and he starts to get ideas."

"Isn't that the point?" Vicky asked, confused.

"No." Luke's stern look intensified. "You should wait until after you're married before you start doing stuff like that."

And he thought she was old-fashioned! "Is that what you do?"

"Well, no, but it's different for me. I'm a detective, not a well-bred young lady."

He sure wasn't. He was one intensely masculine man sprawled across her living room floor looking sexier than she would have believed possible. "That would be fine if this was Boston. But it's Miami. I think this is something I need to know in Miami."

Luke picked up a page and examined it intently. "I don't."

Vicky glowered at his bent head. This was great. He could seduce billions of women if he wanted but he wouldn't help her seduce one man. "All right," she agreed. "If you won't tell me, I'll just have to ask someone else." Some spark of mischief made her add, "Maybe this Spencer..."

Luke's head snapped up. "You're not going around town asking men how to seduce them!"

"I have to ask somebody."

Luke stared at her for a long moment, then clapped a hand to his forehead. "I gotta learn to stay away from you. Every time I talk to you, you get me to do something I don't want to do." He leaned back against the chair and folded his arms. "Okay. What exactly do you want to know?"

Vicky relaxed, happy now that she had his cooperation. "Just a few hints on how to get started. That's all. I mean, how would you go about it?"

Luke closed his eyes. "I can't believe I'm having this conversation."

"If you don't want—"

"I'm trying. I'm trying." He tapped a finger against his bottom lip. "I guess the first step is for the man to get inside. I either invite her over to my place, or wangle an invitation to her place."

Vicky considered that. "So I suppose my step one would be to invite him in."

Luke nodded. "Uh-huh. Ask him in for coffee, tea, a drink, to look at your broken television set, or help you find something you misplaced like your toaster or your emerald ring." He stopped as she picked up her pen and wrote that down. "Don't tell me you're going to take notes?"

"I have to," Vicky said grandly. "It's a habit you get into when you spend most of your life doing research." She gestured with her pen. "Go on."

Luke was still staring at her. "Barney was right," he muttered. "I do need a psychiatrist."

"Luke!"

"All right. All right. Where was I?"

Vicky checked her notes. "Getting him in here."

"Okay." Luke gave the room a quick appraisal. "But before you do that you need to do something about this place. Put on some quiet music. Dim the lights." He gestured at the picture hanging on the opposite wall. "Put a cover over Grampa up there. Grampa staring down at you is a good way to turn someone off."

Vicky took a look at her grandfather's fierce blue eyes and nodded agreement. "That's a good point." She jotted down a note and rested back, imagining the room the way he described. Soft music. Dim lights. No Grampa. She could do this. "Then what?"

Luke squinted his eyes as he thought. "That depends on what reason you used to get him in here. You have to...sort of, uh, go through a ritual of pretending it's a legitimate excuse."

"Okay." Vicky quickly reviewed his excuse list. "I don't own an emerald ring, I never lose my toaster and I don't watch enough television to know if it's working or not. I'd better stick with the coffee one." She wrote it down. "Make coffee. What's next?"

Luke blinked. "Hand him his coffee and sit down next to him."

"What if he's in the chair?"

Luke shook his head. "If he's at all interested, he should have enough sense to have chosen a seat on the sofa."

"Okay." Vicky straightened on the sofa. "Here we are on the sofa. Now what?"

Luke shrugged. "Now you kiss him. Or, if he isn't too obtuse, he kisses you."

Vicky tried to picture the scene and failed. "That won't work. We're both holding cups of scalding coffee. We can't—"

"Then set it down."

"What about him? He's got a cup of coffee, as well."

Luke gave her an impatient look. "Take it away from him."

"I can't."

"Yeah, you can." He scrambled to his feet. "I'll show you."

He settled down beside her. The cushions dipped with his weight, his thigh brushed hers and Vicky tensed. Sitting this close to Luke might not be a good idea. She'd wanted to attack him when he was on the other side of the room. Now he was right beside her. "That's fine. I..."

Luke was busy arranging imaginary cups. "Here," he said as he thrust a pretend mug in her direction. "Pretend you're holding this. I set mine down...like so..." He leaned forward to act out the instructions, then turned to her. "Then I take yours and set it down, too."

His fingertips brushed hers as he took the imaginary cup from her. Her skin tingled from the contact, and the tingle moved through her veins, causing an unexpected increase in her heart rate. Vicky looked at her hands, then up at Luke.

"There, see," he said. "Now you're in a perfect position to kiss him."

That sounded like an excellent idea. *This is Luke, you dummy. He's giving you a lesson!* "You mean like this?" Vicky leaned forward and gave his cheek a brief peck, hoping that would end the whole thing.

It didn't. Luke looked thoroughly disgusted. "No! That's the sort of kiss you give your grandfather—or your grandmother. If you want to seduce someone you have to put some emotion into it. And you have to open your mouth."

Vicky pictured herself lunging toward her date with her mouth wide open. "He'll think I'm going to bite him!"

"You don't open it that wide! You're trying to kiss him, not do a shark imitation. Just open it a little. Like this." Luke opened his mouth a finger-width. "Got it?"

Vicky had something all right. The sight of his parted lips, and the idea of pressing hers against them, was making her body overheat. She was panting, she realized. "Yes, I think so. Like this, right?"

She opened her mouth.

"That's pretty good," said Luke. He stared at her parted lips. "But maybe it would be better if I showed you." He brushed a finger down her cheek, slid his hand around to the back of her neck, lowered his head and stroked his open mouth across hers.

It wasn't anything like kissing Boswell—or if it was, Vicky had forgotten. His lips were warm and moist, and the feel of them seemed to chase every thought she had out of her brain. This would work all right. If she kissed someone like this, they'd definitely end up in the bedroom. Then she forgot about it, giving herself up to the slow stroking of his mouth, while her hands clutched his back and her body lost its muscle. He nibbled gently on her top lip, sucked in her bottom lip, then slowly, easily, unhurriedly slid his tongue between her teeth.

Vicky sagged back. Luke's grip on her tightened, holding her firmly against his hard chest while his tongue moved in and out of her mouth in slow, erotic strokes. Vicky was vaguely aware of one of his hands moving up her torso to close around her breast. His thumb grazed the nipple, causing a jolt of exquisite sensations and there wasn't a thought left in her mind except the way she felt and how much she liked it and how much she wanted it to go on forever.

It didn't. Luke relaxed his grip, and raised his head. Vicky drew in a trembling breath, collapsed back against the cushions and opened her eyes. Luke's face was less than two inches away, his eyes a dusky shade of green, his eyelids half-lowered. Vicky scrambled her brain together, searching for something to say. "Oh," she got out. "So that's, uh, how you do it."

"Uh-huh." Luke's lips moved into a slow, tempting smile. "Do you want me to show you what happens next?"

His hand was on her breast, her heart was beating three thousand beats per second and there were a million other things Vicky wanted him to show her. But common sense reasserted itself. She was supposed to be looking for a husband, not seducing a detective from North Dakota.

She stiffened and moved away. "No," she said. "Thank you. I, uh, think that's enough seduction lessons for one night."

"All right," Luke said easily. He slid back down to the floor and picked up a paper. "If you want to know anything else, just ask."

Vicky was still gathering fragments of her brain from where they'd been scattered during that kiss. "I think I know enough now," she murmured.

Luke looked up at her, frowning. "Hey, just because I told you how to do it doesn't mean you should do it."

Vicky stared at him, nonplussed. "What?"

"You shouldn't! I don't want you seducing Spencer or anyone else without checking with me."

Terrific. She was thinking scandalous thoughts about him, and he was going to pick some other man for her to seduce. Vicky curled back into her original position. "You know, Luke, I think you should meet my mother. You two have a lot in common."

"HER MOTHER!" Luke complained to Barney the next morning.

He slowed the car as they passed a sign directing them to the Kurubla Dog Kennels, which, according to Barney, might be a good place to look for Pumffy clues. "I kissed her and she said I had a lot in common with her mother!"

Barney chuckled. "Well, Luke, old buddy, I'd say that either she's got a real unique family, or you can't kiss worth spit."

Luke ignored him. "I used to be a private detective. Now I'm a dogcatcher and a substitute mother! I don't know what I'm doing wrong."

Barney, the ever helpful, was more than pleased to provide assistance. "Do you want me to give you a list?"

"No," said Luke.

Barney sat back against the seat and did it, anyway. "Your first mistake was agreeing to find her a husband. Then you compounded that by introducing her to a bunch of other men. And your third mistake was not making a move when you're interested in her yourself."

"I'm not interested in her myself!" Luke objected, although he knew that wasn't true. "I just don't like being mistaken for a woman's parent, especially right after I just kissed her."

"Ah." Barney nodded wisely. "You're still in the denial phase."

"I'm not in any phase." Luke took a quick sideways look at Barney's disbelieving expression and sighed. "Look, I am attracted to her but it's just a...a physical thing."

"Uh-huh."

"And even if it wasn't, it wouldn't change anything. Vicky is definitely not interested."

"How do you know?" Barney demanded. "Have you asked her?"

"No." Luke pressed on the brake as they approached a turn. "But she backed off last night. She wants old American heritage with a prestigious career. That's not me."

"You probably just shook her up, that's all. Now that she's had some time to think about it, she'll probably come to her senses and realize that she'd rather have you."

The thought of having Vicky made Luke's foot slip off the brake. She'd certainly looked shocked after that kiss. Then she'd pulled herself together and told him he reminded her of her mother! He yanked the car out of the resulting skid and shook his head. "I don't think so."

"Maybe you should find out for sure." Barney advised. "Give her an option. Make another move and see what happens. That's what I'm going to do with Suzy."

Luke forgot about his problems to focus on Barney's. "You're going to make a move on Suzy?"

"I already did. Granted it was a small one, but the way she reacted—well, I'd say it's time to make another one."

Luke didn't like this. "I don't think that's a good idea, Barney."

"I do. Suzy and I have been spending a lot of time together, what with this Pumffy thing dragging on so long." Barney got that bemused expression on his long face. "She's a special person, Luke. Good-looking. Intelligent. Softhearted..."

"Not to mention manipulative and conniving," Luke muttered under his breath.

"What was that?"

"Nothing." Barney might look innocuous, but he had been a Chicago cop, and he got real defensive when Luke said anything negative about Suzy. Luke didn't want to start an argument—or get a fist in his face—but he didn't want to see his partner hurt, either. "Listen, Barn, you don't want to start something with Suzy. She might be a nice enough person...or she might not be. In any case, she is from a wealthy, socially correct family."

"So?"

"So you're...not."

Barney shrugged. "I don't care about stuff like that. And I'm sure Suzy doesn't, either."

"I'm not so sure." Barney's shoulders stiffened into an ominous warning, and Luke sighed. "What sort of move are you planning on making?"

"The usual type. I'm going to lure her over to my place, grill her a steak and invite her to spend the night."

Luke tried to imagine the elegant Suzy sitting on

Barney's mismatched furniture in his apartment. "At your place? You've got to be kidding."

"Well, it can't happen at her place!" Barney said, disgusted. "Who could seduce someone with all those expensive antiques watching? Not to mention Mrs. Harris."

"Good point," Luke agreed.

"You should try the same thing on Vicky," Barney advised. "Invite her over. Feed her some red meat. Tell her you're crazy about her and show her the bedroom."

The thought of Vicky in his bedroom made Luke a little dizzy. "That wouldn't work with Vicky. She's a vegetarian."

"Then make a salad! What you eat isn't important as long as you make it yourself. Women always get in the mood when a man cooks for them." He chewed on his bottom lip. "Of course I'm going to have to do a darn good steak. Suzy took a pile of cooking courses a couple of years ago."

"You think throwing food at a woman is a good seduction technique?" Luke stopped the car in front of the long, white building that, according to the sign in front, was Kurubla Kennels. "What do they teach you Chicago cops, anyway? Don't you take any courses in subtlety?"

Barney opened his door. "At least I've got moves, which is more than I can say for you. You're busy introducing Vicky to the competition." He climbed out. "The only kind of move, that is, pal, is a dumb one."

10

"SO IF YOU KNOW anything about Pumffy you should tell me now," Luke intoned. "I know you think you're protecting him, but you could easily be making it worse."

The small honey-russet Pomeranian looked deeply into his eyes, then turned her head and pranced off, in a manner that clearly said, "Up yours."

"Thanks for your time," Luke muttered. "And remember what I said. You hear anything, I want to know about it."

He shook his head as he got to his feet and brushed the nonexistent dirt off his knees. "Crazy dog," he muttered. Then he realized what he'd just said and chuckled. Munchkin wasn't the only one who was crazy. After all, he was the one interrogating a dog.

He snagged his drink off the counter and grabbed a canapé from the tray of a passing waiter. Interrogating the dog hadn't been his idea, but it hadn't been Barney's idea, either. His partner had just heard that the Daniels had lost their dog a few days ago, and wanted Luke to ask them about it. Rita Daniels hadn't known much, but she had vaguely suggested he spend a few minutes with Munchkin, who, she'd insisted, was "very observant." She might be right about the observant part, Luke allowed. However, Munchkin wasn't much of a communicator.

He turned toward the door. So much for his assignment to check out the Daniels dog. Now he could check out his other assignment.

He fully expected that to turn out to be a bust, as well. Spencer was a decent enough guy, but he had a number of annoying habits that were bound to set Vicky's teeth on edge. He laughed at almost everything. He'd had his teeth capped, his hair straightened and he was compulsively neat. Plus, no matter where he went, he took his grandmother. If Luke could spot these things, he was sure Vicky could spot them.

Or maybe she'd drag Spencer home and try to seduce him.

Luke was suddenly anxious to get back to her side. He hurried down the hall and into the massive Daniels living room where dozens of socially correct folks were milling around, showing off their new clothes and talking about their new yachts. He'd be glad when this case was over. He was getting tired of hanging around with these folks.

Of course, this case wouldn't end until Vicky found someone. Luke wasn't crazy about that option.

Maybe Barney was right. Maybe he should try something else with Vicky. Maybe if he did, she'd forget about wanting a man with the right background and the right career. Maybe that wasn't as important to her as she thought it was.

He didn't want a socialite, Luke reminded himself. Then again, Vicky wasn't the typical socialite. Perhaps things between them did have a chance of working out.

It didn't take him long to spot Vicky. She was standing beside a fern, wearing an off-white dress with long, lacy sleeves. Even though it was cut low enough to show a tantalizing amount of décolletage, she still looked old-fashioned and a touch too classy for this crowd.

She definitely looked too classy for Spencer. He was standing close to her, his dark head bent in her direction, his teeth flashing white as he smiled. Luke frowned at them. Spencer was looking far too pleased with himself. And Vicky...well, why was she still talking to him, anyway? It had been more than fifteen minutes since he'd introduced them. By now, she should have realized that Spencer wasn't the one, either.

Now she was looking up at him with those big blue eyes. And she was laughing. Luke's spine straightened. She wasn't falling for this guy, was she?

He was about to cross the room to find out what was going on when Vicky handed Spencer her wineglass. A second later Spencer was wandering off through the crowd. Luke knew what that meant. Another one had just bitten the dust. Now the coast was clear for him to take Vicky home, invite himself in for coffee and give her another lesson in seduction—assuming that was what he wanted to do. He felt his body tighten. Yeah, that was what he wanted to do, all right.

He was running through the approach he'd take when Rita Daniels came up to him and put her hand on his arm. "Luke? There's someone here you simply have to meet."

SO MUCH FOR Spencer.

Vicky watched the medium-height, brown-haired man move through the crowd, with her wineglass clutched in his hand. Spencer was easily the best candidate for matrimony she'd met so far. He was good-looking, with a great smile that he'd flashed often. He was clean, he hadn't mentioned her uncle once and he'd even managed to make being a stockbroker sound interesting, which wasn't a simple accomplishment.

So why had she sent him away to find her a drink?

Vicky looked around the room for Luke. He was on the other side of the room, one shoulder propped against the wall while he talked with a sweet-faced red-haired woman. Looking at him made her think about kissing him and that had her perspiring. Good thing she wasn't in that upper-crust finishing school she'd joked about—she would have been expelled for sure for sweating this much.

A square figure dressed in a long flowing gown—lime green and burgundy this time—approached her. "Victoria, darling! I've been looking for you everywhere. I was so pleased when I heard you were here. I've been wondering what happened to you. It's so wonderful to see you again." She looked around. "I have no idea who half these people are."

Vicky doubted that. Madalyne seemed to know the entire world.

"Even Luke's here," Madalyne chatted on. "You remember Luke, don't you? He was at my place a few weeks ago. I'm sure you met him then."

"Yes, I did."

"I haven't had a chance to speak with him yet." She glanced around the room. "You haven't seen him, have you?"

"He's over there." Vicky gestured toward the wall.

"Ah yes, I see him. He's talking with Sarah Smothers—the nanny for the Daniels. Don't they make a nice couple?"

"Nanny?" Vicky eyed the woman. "That woman is a nanny?"

"Yes. She's very nice. The Daniels were lucky to get her."

"Were they?" Vicky narrowed her eyes. That woman would look good in black stockings and a garter belt. She'd probably even wear them.

"Wouldn't it be splendid if they got together?" Madalyne bubbled. "Luke deserves someone like that—especially after what Darlene did to him."

"Darlene?"

Madalyne looked shocked. "You haven't heard about Luke and Darlene? My dear, where have you been?"

"Mostly in my lab." Vicky kept watching Luke and the redhead. She was smiling. Luke was smiling. Vicky wanted to kill them both.

Madalyne went on gossiping. "Well, Luke and Darlene were quite an item a couple of years ago. They seemed so compatible. Everyone thought they were one step away from picking a date."

"Oh?" He looked darn close to picking a date with the redhead. That was fine. Luke should date, although Vicky didn't know when he was going to fit it in. He should be finding a husband for her, not picking up women.

Madalyne continued with her story. "Then Darlene broke it off and married Edgar Snow." She snorted. "We couldn't understand it. Not that there's anything wrong with Edgar. He's a decent enough sort." Madalyne raised her wineglass to her lips. "Although if you ask me, he can't hold a candle to Luke." She lowered her voice confidentially. "To be perfectly honest, dear, I've always suspected that money was the motivating factor in Darlene's decision. She was always after Luke to take a job in her father's company. But he wasn't interested in doing that."

"Of course, he wouldn't be." Luke was interested in finding lost kids, not making lots of money.

"The story I heard was that they had something of a row. Darlene's father made Luke a generous offer and Luke turned it down. The next thing we knew, Luke was out of the picture and Darlene was dating Edgar."

"Really?"

"I personally think she made a big mistake," Madalyne announced. "Luke is a tremendously fine person. He might not be from a wealthy family, but he's a good man."

"He certainly is." Vicky agreed. He was a wonderful man. He deserved to be happy.

Unfortunately, the idea of him being happy with that nanny made her physically ill.

"ALL RIGHT, lay it on me," Luke said as he drove her home later. "What was the matter with Spencer?"

He's too tall, when he smiles he shows too many teeth and his eyes don't crinkle at the corners. He has blue eyes, not green eyes, he smiles far too much, he was wearing a lime green shirt and when he touched my hand I didn't feel anything. "Nothing," said Vicky.

"Nothing?" Luke repeated.

"No. I don't think there is anything wrong with Spencer." She'd come to that decision after watching Luke chat with the sweet-faced nanny in the corner.

There was no denying her reaction. She'd been jealous. Jealous wasn't good. She knew she didn't have a future with Luke. He was not the right one for her, and she was definitely not the right one for him. But she'd been wickedly, violently jealous.

That could only mean one thing. She was getting too attached to Luke. She was dreaming about him. She was thinking about him. She was remembering their kiss. And she was not concentrating on finding a husband. She needed to put an end to this. She'd met lots of men who would thrill her parents. It was time she picked one and got this husband business settled. Once she'd done that, Luke would be out of her life, and that would be a good thing.

Right. And it would also be a good thing if all her experiments failed and she never found the right mix of fertilizer and genetics and her lab was filled with dead vegetables tomorrow when she went in. "As a matter of fact, I really liked him."

Luke looked over at her in surprise. "You did?"

"Yes." She had liked him. She hadn't been attracted to him, but she hadn't minded him.

Luke cleared his throat. "I thought he seemed a little frivolous. All those jokes about open-heart surgery..."

Vicky didn't think open-heart surgery was something to laugh about, either, but... "I think that's just a...a nervous reaction."

"He did seem a little on the nervous side." Luke shifted. "Sometimes people like that have something to hide."

Those jerky little motions had driven her crazy. "I'm sure Spencer doesn't. After all, you did check him out, didn't you?"

"Yes, I did, but there's always the chance that I missed something."

"I wouldn't think so." Vicky took a deep breath. She could do this, if she set her mind to it. "He does have all the other things I'm looking for. His heredity is impeccable. As a matter of fact, I think his great-great-grandfather probably knew mine—on my mother's side, of course."

"Maybe so, but—"

"He's got a sense of humor, he's very interested in ecology and he doesn't do a lot of entertaining. And he's certainly got a nice grandmother."

"Very nice," Luke agreed absently. "But, uh, don't you think it odd that he takes her everywhere he goes?"

"No," Vicky said, although she did. "I think he's just...considerate." She stared straight ahead, into the lights of the oncoming traffic. "Of course, I'll have to spend a little more time with him...get to know him better...but I really think that you've done it this time. I think this is the one." She forced a lighthearted, excited tone, hoping it would make her feel lighthearted and excited, as well. "Isn't this terrific?"

"Yeah, it's great," Luke said in a dull tone. "Just...great."

"GREAT?"

Barney shoved a hand through his mop of black hair and stared at Luke out of dark eyes that clearly said, "You are insane." "She told you she'd found a husband and you said it was great?" He shook his head. "I was right about you. You do need a psychiatrist."

Luke glared across the office at him. "You're the one

who's been running all over the city looking for a dog that's not lost and you think I need a psychiatrist?"

"I'm looking for a dognapper! Which reminds me. Did you find out anything about the Daniels dog?"

"Munchkin? No, he just got away from the nanny when she took him and the Daniels boy for a walk." She had said something about seeing a dark-haired fellow with a tattoo on his arm approach the dog, but when she'd confronted him, he'd given the dog back. There wasn't anything suspicious about that! "You're looking for a dognapper that doesn't exist, Barn! And it is great that Vicky finally found someone." Just like it would be great if space aliens swooped out of the sky and destroyed the entire planet. "That's what she hired me to do—to find her a husband. It looks like I did it. Now I won't have to do it anymore. I can concentrate on some real cases. She'll pay her bill, and maybe you'll be so thrilled about that you'll stop worrying about this Pumffy thing."

"I'll worry about Pumffy until I find him," Barney said, unperturbed. "Right now, I'm worried about you."

"Barney..."

"You're acting like an idiot, Luke! Instead of saying, 'Oh, great, you've found some other guy,' why didn't you tell her that Spencer's got some weird granny fetish and she'd be better off climbing into bed with you?"

Luke thought about Vicky climbing into his bed and took a deep breath. "That's not what this is about," he reminded them both. He gave Barney a suspicious look. "Just a minute. How do you know Spencer's got a weird granny fetish?"

Barney shrugged. "Suzy told me this morning."

Luke checked his watch. "You saw Suzy this morning?"

"I couldn't help it." Barney looked smug and masculine and superior. "I just rolled over and there she was."

"Ah. I gather the great seduction scene worked."

"Not exactly the way I planned." Barney's lips moved into a slow, satisfied smile. "She walked in, I gave her a glass of wine, told her we were having marinated steak and she said, 'The steaks are going to wait because I can't.'" His grin widened. "That was pretty much that. Easiest seduction I've ever done. It didn't do much for the steaks, though. By the time we got around to them, they'd almost disintegrated."

"So now you're sleeping with Mrs. Harris's little girl." Luke shook his head. "That's a bad move, Barn. I warned you about her. She's—"

Barney's smile vanished. "Don't you start in on Suzy. She's a terrific lady."

And one of these days she could very well dump him for a ticket to Europe, or a guy with a lot more money. Luke passed a hand over his face a few times. He didn't want his friend to get hurt, but he didn't think he could do much about it now except cross his fingers and hope it didn't happen. "I suppose this means you're going to keep looking for that stupid dog of hers?"

"No," said Barney. "*We're* looking for that stupid dog of hers." He lowered his voice. "I've got a hot tip."

"On a dog?" Luke snorted. "How do you get a hot tip on a dog?"

"It's not easy," Barney complained. "You wouldn't

believe how much I had to pay for this tip. It makes me wish I was back in Chicago. The winters are hell, but you can usually get a blue light special on informants."

"Barney..."

"Just pay attention, Luke." He took a look around the office, as if making sure there were no other ears listening. "My informant tells me that he ran across this character in a bar a week or so ago. He mentioned something about a dog racket going on at the place he worked."

"A dog racket?"

"Yeah. They're snatching well-bred dogs and using them for breeding purposes." Barney lowered his voice to a whispery growl. "I understand they're planning on selling the puppies on the black market."

"The black market?" The whole world had gone insane. First Vicky fell for Spencer. Then Barney got hot and heavy with Suzy, an experience which seemed to have drained all sense from his brain. "I doubt that there's a black market for dogs."

"There is, and it's a lucrative one, too." He got to his feet. "My informant is going to meet us tonight and point out this character to us."

"Us?" Luke asked.

"Yeah. I figured you'd want to come along."

"Do I have to?" Luke asked plaintively. "I'm not really in the mood."

"The air will do you good. So would a good dose of common sense, but, unfortunately, it's not something I can pick up at the drugstore for you." He started for the door. "Are you in, or am I going to perish in the streets because you weren't around to back me up?"

Luke gave in. "I supposed I'd better. With my luck,

something would happen to you, and I'd feel eternally responsible."

"HIS NAME IS SPENCER," Vicky told Gina. "He's, uh, related to Paul Revere or something and, uh..." She struggled to think of something wonderful to say about Spencer. "And he's very nice," she concluded.

"Nice?" Gina yawned into a hand. "What does that mean? Does it mean that when you look at him you want to jump him or does it mean that when you look at him you think, 'Yup, he's a nice guy. He should make my toes tingle, but he doesn't'?"

It was probably more of the latter, but Vicky wasn't sharing that with Gina. She'd made up her mind and she wasn't backing out now. "That's not important. He's everything I want in a man. Besides, I really like his grandmother."

"Grandmother?" Gina looked shocked. "You're considering spending the rest of your life with someone because of their grandmother?"

"It's not just that! Besides, grandmothers are important. My grandmother will like his grandmother. They have a lot in common. As a matter of fact, my entire family will be thrilled with Spencer!"

"And what about you?" Gina demanded. "Are you thrilled with Spencer?"

Vicky hesitated. "He's very clean. And he laughs a lot." He did laugh a lot. He'd even laughed when she'd talked about her sea-vegetation project. "Sea vegetables," he'd said. "That's hysterical, Vicky! Are all the gardeners in North America going to have to buy scuba diving equipment?" At the time, she'd laughed politely, but she hadn't appreciated the joke. Was he going to spend all his life laughing at her work?

She dropped a book on her desk a little too hard. There she went, being picky again. "He's a terrific person and I like him a lot."

"Right," said Gina, but she didn't look convinced.

Vicky wasn't convinced, either. She would be after tonight, though. She'd kiss him. Bells would go off. She'd start feeling like ripping off Spencer's clothes instead of ripping off Luke's clothes. This matter would be settled, her parents would be happy and she could finally get on with her work.

She stuffed another test tube into the holder. That better be how it worked! If it didn't, she was in big trouble.

"I DON'T KNOW HOW MUCH you offered for him to point out the suspect, but my guess is that it wasn't enough," Luke advised.

He slouched down into the mauve couch in Barney's apartment, with his feet stacked up on the coffee table. This had to be the worst day of his life. Vicky was spending the evening with Spencer. He'd wasted the whole day waiting for an informant who didn't show. He was hot. He was tired. He was miserable.

"I guess not." Barney took a swallow out of the beer can in his hand, and dropped his head back against the cushions. "The guy did seem keen on talking to me. I wonder what went wrong."

"I've been wondering that all day." Luke slid lower into the chair. When had his life gone wrong? It hadn't seemed that bad yesterday. Of course, yesterday Vicky hadn't met Spencer. That was the low point. Introducing her to Spencer had been a dumb idea. Kissing her had been a dumb idea, too. Sleeping with her would also have been a dumb idea. He knew that. His body just hadn't figured it out yet.

"Suzy's real disappointed, too," Barney went on. "She was hoping this would pan out."

"Uh-huh." Luke had listened to Barney's end of the phone conversation he'd just had with Suzy. The number of times he'd heard "Don't worry, honey" and "We'll find him sooner or later, sweetheart" had made him a little nauseous, and increased his misery.

Barney cleared his throat. "You know, Luke, I'm really starting to wonder about this dog thing." He rolled the beer can between his palms. "Sometimes I think I'm never going to find Pumffy."

"You'll find him," said Luke. "As soon as Suzy gets her trip to Europe, he'll magically turn up."

"She's not going to do that," Barney insisted. "This thing with Pumffy has really shaken her up. She says its time she made some changes in her life. She's tired of drifting around. She just wants to settle down and raise dogs."

"Uh-huh." Luke had his doubts about that, but there was no point in saying anything to Barney. Besides, there was a faint chance that Luke was wrong about this. He crossed his fingers. He hoped he was wrong about this. If he wasn't, Barney had a hard fall in front of him when the truth came out.

Unfortunately, Luke hadn't been wrong about much. When he'd first met Vicky he'd suspected she was only interested in superficialities. It looked as if that was the case. Spencer sure didn't have a lot going for him—except for his background and his career and his fingernails, of course.

Barney roused himself. "Oh, speaking of Suzy, she mentioned something just now that you might find interesting."

Luke groaned. "If it's another hot tip on a dognapper, I don't want to hear it."

"It isn't. It's about that Spencer fellow you set Vicky up with."

"Oh, him." The man Luke wanted to take apart inch by inch. "What about him?"

"Suzy took an actuarial accounting course with him."

Luke had thought he was past the point of being surprised by anything Suzy had done—but he was wrong. "Suzy studied actuarial accounting?"

Barney nodded confirmation. "For one semester. Then she realized accounting wasn't in her karma."

"Accounting isn't in anyone's karma, but I don't see—"

"That's not all. According to Suzy, this Spencer character has something of a scandalous past."

Luke straightened at that. "He does?"

"Uh-huh." Barney grinned. "It's not quite what you and I would think is scandalous, but it might not be something Ms. Vicky and family would approve of, either."

"I, UH...DON'T KNOW if I can see you again," Vicky told Spencer. "There's a...a chance that I might be going to South America."

She wrinkled her nose as she closed the door behind him. *You shouldn't have said that, Victoria. You're not go-*

ing to South America and there is nothing wrong with Spencer. He's a nice man with a nice grandmother, remember?

He was also a man who got a failing grade in kissing.

She hung up her coat, went into her living room and sat down in the middle of the sofa. The room was arranged just the way Luke had described. Soft music on the stereo. Lights dimmed. Grandfather's picture safely tucked away, replaced with a landscape she'd had in her bedroom. She'd even had the coffeepot set up so she just had to switch it on.

She hadn't needed any of it because the second she'd kissed Spencer, she'd realized that she couldn't seduce him.

At least she hadn't had to wait until after dinner to find out. She'd found out as soon as Spencer arrived to pick her up. "Hi," he'd said. Then he'd bent his head and brushed his lips across hers. Vicky had closed her eyes and kissed him back. She hadn't been naive enough to expect his kiss to affect her the way Luke's had, but she had thought that something would happen. A tingle. A spark. Anything.

It hadn't. She hadn't felt repulsed by Spencer. She hadn't felt attracted to Spencer. She simply hadn't felt anything.

It had been exactly like kissing Spencer's grandmother—or her own.

Spencer hadn't appeared to have the same problem. He raised his head and touched her cheek and his eyes sparkled at her, and Vicky felt almost sick with disappointment. She'd finally found a man who was perfect, who seemed to want to get hot and heavy with her, and she couldn't do it.

She'd spent the remainder of their date trying to tell

herself that it didn't matter, that it wasn't important and that there were a lot of things she liked about Spencer, but it hadn't helped. As a matter of fact, she'd had a hard time remembering the things she did like about him. Everything he did, from the way he put salt on his potatoes, to the way he held his napkin, irritated her.

"Don't be picky!" she ordered herself. Spencer was a pleasant man, her parents would approve, and the fact that he did nothing for her libido was a minor consideration. Tomorrow she would call him, explain that she was *not* going to South America, and that she would love to see him again. Maybe if she spent a few more evenings with him, he would kick-start her libido.

Somehow, she doubted that would happen.

She'd just switched on the coffee pot when someone knocked at her door. *Luke*, she thought, but then she realized that of course it wasn't Luke. He didn't have any reason to come over now.

She took a look through the peephole. It was Luke.

"I've been trying to reach you all evening," he complained when she opened the door. "Where were you?"

"Having dinner with Spencer." Why couldn't she have the same reaction to Spencer that she had to Luke? Just looking at him made her think about kissing him. Kissing him and hugging him. Kissing him, hugging him and ripping off his clothes and putting her hands on his body.

"Oh." He peered over her head. "Is he still here?"

"No. He left." She gave her head a side-to-side shake

to clear it. "What are you doing here, Luke? Has something happened?"

"Not really." He rubbed the back of his neck with one hand. "I just, uh, found out something about Spencer that I thought you should know."

Vicky couldn't think of anything she wanted to know about Spencer. "What's that?"

"It seems that he doesn't have an unblemished past, after all."

"He doesn't?" Spencer had looked pretty unblemished. It wasn't a look that turned her on, but...

"No. Apparently he was kicked out of university. Something about cheating on an exam."

"Spencer cheated on an exam?" Vicky tried to reconcile that with the man she'd just had dinner with. Come to think of it, his eyes had looked a little shifty. And he'd taken the last dinner roll without asking her if she wanted it.

Luke nodded. "I don't know if it makes a difference but I thought you should know. In case it does, I mean."

"It does make a difference." Vicky sagged against the wall, relieved. Thank you, thank you, thank you. Her parents wouldn't approve of Spencer. She couldn't marry him. She didn't have to seduce him!

"I'm sorry it turned out that way," said Luke. "I mean, I know you liked him and he did seem to have all the things you were looking for, but..."

Vicky felt weak with euphoria. "No, no, that's fine. Really. I'd rather find out now than after I...that is, after it was too late."

Luke took a step closer to peer into her face. "Are you sure you're all right? You look a little upset."

Vicky roused herself to focus on him. He was standing in the doorway, his hair rumpled, not wearing a tie or a suit and his forehead was furrowed with worry. "I'm not upset, Luke. I, uh, didn't like him that much after all, and, well, I'm...just...grateful, that's all." She was grateful. Grateful that Spencer was gone. Grateful that she didn't have to practice her newly acquired seduction technique on him when the only person she wanted to seduce was Luke.

She straightened. "Would you like a cup of coffee?"

Luke was still looking concerned. "Sure, but—"

"I'll get it." Vicky tottered into the kitchen and pulled two cups from the cupboard. Her brain seemed to be stuck on stun. All she could think about was Luke. Luke's mouth. Luke's hands. Luke's body. *Get a grip, Victoria.*

She was pouring coffee into the second cup when Luke wandered into the kitchen. "What happened to Grampa?" he demanded.

Vicky fixated on the patch of skin revealed by his open-necked shirt. "Who?"

"Your grandfather's picture. It's missing from the living room."

"Oh, that." Vicky handed him a cup. "I put it in the den."

"You did, huh?" Luke took a sip of coffee and eyed her over the rim. "How come?"

Good question. "I, uh..."

"Don't tell me you were planning on seducing Spencer?" His eyes narrowed. "Or did you already do it?"

I was going to but I didn't. "No, of course not."

"Good thing," Luke muttered. Suddenly, he set down his cup, stretched out an arm and pulled her to him. Then he was kissing her, rubbing his mouth over hers, holding her against him. Vicky released a sigh and leaned against him, reveling in the pleasure of his mouth, his tongue, every inch of his body pressing against hers.

Luke raised his head, but kept his arms firmly around her, and looked into her eyes. "I'm glad you didn't seduce Spencer."

"So am I." She stroked a hand along his cheek. "I did think about it but I couldn't do it. I didn't get past seduction lesson number one, remember?"

"Oh, yeah." He exhaled slowly. "Well, you know what I think?"

"What?"

"I think it's time for lesson number two."

A jumble of thoughts flashed across Vicky's mind. He wasn't right for her. He had the wrong background and the wrong career and her parents would never approve...and she ached all over because she wanted him so much.

"I think you're right," Vicky said firmly.

LUKE TOOK HER into the living room. The bedroom would have been a more logical place, but the living room was closer and he needed to sit down. He dropped into the green plaid armchair—the one that had been her grandfather's—and drew her down into his lap, clutching her against him. She hadn't seduced Spencer. She was curled up against him, her mouth warm and willing under his, and all he wanted to do was strip off her clothes and take her hard and fast so she'd never think of another man again. *Go slow, Luke.*

She doesn't have a lot of experience with this. You want to make it great for her.

Vicky straightened and looked at him, her eyes widely innocent and wickedly tempting at the same time. "I thought we were supposed to be on the sofa."

Luke cleared his throat. "This is lesson two. It happens in a new venue. The armchair."

"Oh." She made a motion as if to rise. "In that case, maybe I should get my notebook."

Luke tightened his grip. "No need for that. I'll make sure you remember."

"All right." She settled back. "Am I supposed to be doing something or..."

Luke cleared his throat. "Yeah, uh, well, uh, now you should suggest that it's getting warm in here."

Vicky nodded. "It is getting warm in here but I don't..." She paused when Luke unfastened a couple of buttons on his shirt. "Oh, now I get it."

"Right," said Luke. His hand went to her blouse, but instead of undoing it, he closed his palm over a breast, then scraped a thumb over the hardening nipple. Vicky gasped. "You like that?" Luke murmured.

"Hmmm." She arched her back, pushing her breast against his hand. Luke molded material around the nipple, feeling it rise further. Then he bent forward and closed his lips around it. Vicky moaned and her fingers went to her own buttons. "Should I..."

"Definitely," Luke agreed.

She started working on the buttons. As soon as she had a few undone, Luke slid his hands through the opening, across the softest skin he'd ever felt and unfastened her bra. He eased the blouse down off her shoulders, taking her bra with it, then he rested back, drinking in the sight of her, sitting half-naked on his lap.

Vicky stirred restlessly. "Luke?"

"Hmmm?"

"Is something wrong?"

"Wrong?" Luke couldn't think of anything that was wrong in the entire galaxy. "No, nothing's wrong."

"Good," said Vicky. "Because you're looking awfully warm." She moistened her lips, undid the rest of the buttons on his shirt and splayed her palms across his chest.

Luke groaned at the sensation. He cupped her breasts, teasing nipples with his fingers, pulled her closer so he could repeat the exercise with his tongue. Vicky's deep-throated gasps of delighted approval increased his arousal to almost painful proportions. He took his hands off her and dragged in a couple of ragged breaths in an attempt to calm himself down. Vicky looked at him, her face foggy with desire. "Now what?"

"Now we move to the floor," Luke decided. He straightened and slid down off the chair, onto the carpet, taking her with him, lowering her onto her back. When he pushed up her skirt and pressed the heel of his hand against the juncture of her thighs, she arched her hips up to meet him. Her eyelids drifted closed, her breathing became short, quick pants, interspersed with appreciative sounds of pleasure. Luke fingered the waistband of her panty hose, then tugged them down off her hips, and placed his lips where his hand had been.

Vicky gave a strangled moan and instinctively started to close her legs. Luke held them open with his hands, licking his tongue up inside her, while she writhed against him and whispered his name. "Luke. Oh, my goodness, that feels good. Yes...oh, yes." Then her hands were in his hair, and her voice was thicker. "Luke...please..."

Luke raised his head and looked down her length. She was stretched out on the carpet half-naked, her hair tumbled around her head. The eyes that looked at him were heavy-lidded and hazy and questioning. Luke took a breath. "At this point...or at any point you want, you can stop this. You just say, 'I think that's enough.'" He paused, waiting, but Vicky didn't say anything. "Or you can say, 'I think we should take this into the bedroom.'"

Vicky sat up, clutching her discarded blouse against her chest. Luke was sitting back on his heels, looking at her. His eyes were the darkest green she'd ever seen, the passion and desire in them as easy to read as a first-year chemical analysis test. He was fully aroused and he wanted her, but if she said that it was enough, he'd sit up, help her dress and treat the entire episode as if it had been a learning experience. Her body ached with need, but it was the swelling of her heart in her chest as she gazed into his face that convinced Vicky. She forgot all about his heritage, his unfortunate North Dakota connection and his less than respectable profession. "I think we should take this into the bedroom," she whispered.

Luke released a breath. "So do I." Then he was on his feet, helping her up, his arm locking around her waist. "Let's go."

They stopped once in the hallway to exchange a steamy kiss and again at the bedroom door. Luke released her and started stripping off his clothes, his gaze never leaving her body. Vicky's skirt was still bunched around her waist—she shoved it off and stepped out of it, then sank down on the bed and watched him tug off his jeans, then remove his briefs as well and kick them away. "Okay?" he asked.

"Oh, yes," Vicky breathed, entranced by the sight of him.

"Good." He tugged her to her feet and kissed her again, and she was touching him, holding him, feeling his hardness against her, pushing between her thighs. They fell onto the bed together, clutching each other, rolling to find a good position. He shifted sideways, parting her legs, sliding a finger up inside her while Vicky surged up against his hand, gasping with pleasure. Then finally, finally, he was moving over her, pushing into her, hard and heavy and soft and tender, all at the same time. She held on to his shoulders while he raised her hips to meet his, then pushed farther and farther inside until she couldn't stand it anymore. She arched up against him, shuddering into climax while he thrust again and again until he did the same.

"ARE YOU POSITIVE you've never seduced anyone before?" Luke asked the next morning.

He sat at Vicky's kitchen table, drinking coffee, his hair damp from his shower, wearing the same clothes he'd had on last night. Vicky found herself wondering if she could announce that it was warm in here and drag him back into the bedroom. "You seem to be awfully good at it."

"I must have a natural aptitude," Vicky said demurely. "Not to mention an excellent teacher." She was astonished herself at how natural it had been with Luke—how satisfying...and how addictive. She didn't have any questions about her libido this morning. If it was still functioning after the night they'd spent together, then there was nothing wrong with it.

"Of course." Luke drained his coffee cup. "I'd better get to the office before Barney notices I'm missing and starts looking for me." He grinned. "With his track record it'd take him six weeks to find me." He stopped in front of her to give her a swift kiss that deepened into a longer kiss. Luke finally broke it off, groaned and released her. "If we keep that up, neither of us will ever get to work."

That didn't sound too bad. Vicky would gladly skip a day of work to spend it with him—even if it would delay her research.

Luke started for the door. "I'll see you tonight, then." He stopped and looked at her, his brow furrowed with concern. "I will see you tonight, won't I? Or was this just a one-night seduction?"

Vicky shook her head. She wasn't sure what it was, but it was definitely not a one-night thing. She supposed it came under the heading of a fling.

Luke's anxious look vanished. "I didn't think so." He shrugged on his jacket. "I guess this means I'm out of a job, hmmm?"

"What?"

"The husband hunting thing." He grinned widely. "That's one case I'm happy not to solve."

"Someone's going to have to solve it," Vicky murmured, but Luke was already out the door.

11

"NO, I HAVEN'T FOUND anyone yet," Vicky confessed to her mother a week later. "I've been too busy lately to spend much time on that."

"Oh?" Her mother sighed a tired, resigned sigh. "What's keeping you so busy, Victoria? Is it your work?"

"Not...entirely." Vicky took a peek around the bedroom door. Luke was standing, stark naked, beside the bed, humming a cheerful tune as he dried off from his shower. *There's a naked man in my bedroom. I'm having an affair with him and it's a little difficult to look for a husband under those circumstances.* "I mean, yes, it is my work, Mother. My research is, uh, at a critical stage."

"I see." There was another sigh. "Well, I know how important that is to you, dear. But it would be so nice if you could find someone."

"I'm sure I will," Vicky said vaguely. "I just can't fit it in right now."

She wrinkled her nose as she replaced the phone in its cradle. She must be a late bloomer. Most people started lying to their parents when they were teenagers. She'd waited until she was thirty! Maybe that's why she was doing so much of it lately.

Either that, or it was one of the side-effects of having a fling.

"I THINK I'M TURNING into a compulsive liar," she told Gina that afternoon. "Yesterday I told Dr. Ridgeway that I hadn't finished designing the sea-carrot nutrient experiments when actually I finished two days ago but haven't written them up yet. And this morning, I told my mother I was too busy with work to find a husband." She stretched back and rubbed her eyes. "I suppose turning into a compulsive liar is one of the downsides of leading a decadent life."

She said the last part with a sense of amazement. She, Dr. Victoria Sommerset-Hayes, was leading a decadent life. If she'd known it was going to be this much fun, she would have done it years ago.

Gina pouted her full lips together. "I'm afraid what you're doing doesn't qualify as a decadent life-style, Vicky. A decadent life-style is when you spend all day at the bar and go home every night with a different man. You spend all day here, and only go home with Luke."

That sounded pretty scandalous to Vicky. "That's true. But if my parents knew about Luke I'm sure they'd think it was decadent."

"You haven't told them about him yet, huh?" Gina crossed her legs, exposing a large amount of thigh. "When are you planning on doing that? Before the first grandchild or after the fifth?"

Vicky gave her a derisive look. "I'm not planning on telling them at all."

"Don't you think you should?"

"No," said Vicky. "How exactly would I put it? Oh, by the way, Mother, I'm having an affair with a detective from North Dakota?" She thought about her mother's reaction and shuddered. "I don't think so."

"You're going to have to tell them sooner or later."

"Why?" Vicky asked, surprised at the suggestion. "Would you tell your parents you were having a fling?"

Gina's eyes widened. "Absolutely not. My parents might be from Nebraska, but they don't approve of flings any more than parents from Boston. However, I would tell them if it was serious."

"So would I." Vicky flipped open her notebook. "But this isn't serious."

Gina blinked. "It looks pretty serious to me."

"It isn't. It's just a fling." Granted, it didn't feel like a fling. At times—most of the time in fact—it felt pretty darn serious. But then again, what did she know about flings?

Gina slid off her stool. "How about Luke? Does he know this is just a fling?"

"Of course, he does," Vicky said stoutly. They hadn't discussed it, but she assumed he realized this was an affair. "He knows the qualities I need in a man. Besides, he's never said anything about it being serious."

"That doesn't mean anything. Men don't ever tell you what they're thinking. They just leap to the illogical conclusion that if you're spending every waking moment with them, you're serious."

"Luke understands the situation. I told him about it a long time ago."

Gina lowered her perfectly groomed eyebrows. "I don't know, Vicky. You two have all the symptoms of a couple in it pretty deep. You talk about him, you think about him, you get gooey-eyed whenever I mention his name—and Luke acts the same way. I think you're both in over your heads."

Vicky swallowed. Gina wasn't saying anything she hadn't noticed herself. It was a normal reaction, though—the way people were supposed to feel when they had an affair. "That doesn't mean either of us is serious."

"I don't see it that way." Gina patted her shoulder. "And I don't think Luke sees it that way, either."

"Sure he does." Just because they hadn't talked about it didn't mean Luke didn't understand. They just had other things to talk about. Besides, Luke was busy. He was doing something with Barney, he'd been called in on a missing person case, there had been a runaway teen, a husband had disappeared...

And there had been her. She hadn't been thinking about her manhunting project, either. She'd been busy with her work, and she'd been busy with Luke. She flushed as she thought about all the ways that they'd been busy. None of them had involved finding another man.

Not that she wanted another man—at least, not at this point. But someday she was going to have to get back to doing that. Luke knew that as well as she did.

"DO YOU HAVE TO BE so relentlessly cheerful all the time?" Barney grumbled.

He wandered into Luke's office and dropped, in his usual boneless manner, into his favorite chair. "All this whistling. Smiling. Laughing. You don't even talk to your phone anymore. It's starting to get on my nerves."

Luke looked up from a folder on his latest runaway

kid case and grinned at his partner. "Sorry. I'll, uh, try to be my usual crabby self." He made a valiant effort to force his lips into a suitably dour expression. It wasn't easy. His life was ticking along nicely. He'd spent every night since the Spencer episode with Vicky—and it wasn't because he was trying to find her a husband, either. That topic hadn't come up, and Luke didn't expect it ever would—except when they got around to discussing the next step of their relationship. Then he'd have to deal with her parents. He put that thought aside and concentrated on other things, like minivans with three little girls in the back seat.

"You're doing it again," Barney growled.

Luke gave up and let his smile widen. "You'll just have to get used to it, Barn. Besides, I'm supposed to be cheerful. I'm the cheerful one in this partnership. You're the one who looks like a gangster, so you have to look morose."

"No problem," said Barney.

Luke suddenly realized Barney was looking more morose than usual. "What's wrong? Do you have another hot tip on Suzy's missing dog?"

"Nope." Barney's long face drooped. "And I don't think I'm going to be getting any, either. As a matter of fact, I'm thinking of giving up looking for Pumffy altogether."

"Oh?" Come to think of it, Barney hadn't asked him to do something dumb in the past twenty-four hours. "Why's that? Pumffy hasn't rematerialized, has he?"

Barney laced his fingers together and studied them. "No, he hasn't. But I wouldn't be surprised if he did real soon. Maybe right around the time Suzy leaves for Europe."

Luke stiffened. "Suzy's going to Europe?"

"Apparently so. Her father gave her tickets to Paris yesterday—along with tickets to Greece, Spain, Italy...and London. He said he thought it might take her mind off Pumffy."

Luke searched for something to say. "I thought Suzy was tired of traveling around."

"So did I," said Barney.

Luke cleared his throat. "Well, uh, maybe her father is right. Maybe a trip would take her mind off Pumffy."

Barney glowered fiercely. "I don't care if he's right. I don't want her to go to Europe. I want her to stay here with me."

"Did you, uh, tell her that?"

"No," Barney admitted. "I told her it was up to her. Then I said that I'd keep looking for Pumffy while she was gone, and she said I shouldn't bother—that she was sure Pumffy would turn up sooner or later." He looked miserable. "It looks like you were right about her."

"You never know," said Luke, watching him. "It's not like Pumffy turned up. Maybe he has been dognapped and Suzy's, uh, just trying to cope with the enormity of his loss."

Barney shoved a hand through his shaggy hair. "You don't really believe that, do you?"

Luke hesitated. He didn't believe that, but it didn't mean he was right. "Well, uh..."

"I'm not sure I do, either," Barney said glumly.

"I NEED TO FIND a dog and I need to find it now," Luke told Vicky that evening.

He sat on the floor of her living room, with his back propped against the sofa and a piece of pizza in his hand. "I think it's the only thing that'll save Barney."

"Oh?" Vicky took a piece of pizza from the box and leaned back beside him, alternately worrying that he didn't understand the situation, and wishing she was tasting him instead of this mushroom-and-cheese combination. Miami was definitely a bad influence on her. Not only had she become a compulsive liar, but she was also turning into a nymphomaniac! "What's the matter with Barney?"

"Suzy." Luke looked glum. "Suzy and that darn dog of hers. That's what's the matter with Barney." He produced a small shadow of his usually cheerful, crinkly-eyed smile. "And probably the fact that he's from Chicago. We mustn't forget that."

"I suppose." Vicky straightened and dragged her mind off Luke's body. He was from North Dakota. That was something she mustn't forget.

Luke patted her shoulder. "That was a joke, Vicky." He set down his pizza and let his head fall back against the sofa cushions. "To be honest, I think Barney's real problem is me."

"You?"

"Yeah, me. I've convinced him that Suzy was just using him." He opened his eyes. "I did think she was, but, well, now I'm not so sure. I could be wrong about her." He gestured in her direction. "Look how wrong I was about you."

"About me?" Vicky pulled another piece of pizza out of the box. "You mean about me being old-fashioned?"

"No. I was right about that. You are old-fashioned."

If he knew what she was thinking he wouldn't say that. "I am?"

Luke held up a hand. "Hey, I didn't say I didn't like it. As a matter of fact, it's one of the things I like about you. No, make that one of the millions of things I like about you."

Their gazes met, his eyes, his entire expression, brimming with affection. Vicky's stomach lurched. Could Gina be right? Was Luke in too deep? And was the answering burst of affection she'd felt an indication that she was in too deep, as well?

She wrenched her gaze away and focused back on her food. "How were you wrong about me, then?" she asked, to stop herself from thinking.

"Hmmm? Oh." Luke shrugged. "I thought you were another shallow socialite who just wanted a husband with the right breeding, the right career, the right bank account." He rolled his eyes, disgusted with himself. "Boy, was I wrong."

Vicky steeled herself. "Only about the shallow part. You're right about the rest."

Luke angled his head to look down at her. "What?"

She tried to look nonchalant. "Well, you are. Those are the qualities I need in a man. A husband, that is."

Luke shrugged that off. "I know that's what you used to want, but—"

"It still is, Luke." Vicky set down her now-cold piece of pizza and faced him. "I need a husband who has the right background and the right career. That's why I hired you."

Luke blinked. "I know that. But surely you aren't still expecting me to do that."

"Well, no." Vicky gave a nervous laugh. "At least,

not right now. That would be a little...bizarre. But sooner or later I'm going to have to find one."

Luke closed his eyes. When he opened them they were the coldest green she'd ever seen. "What about us? Are you telling me that our relationship doesn't have a future?"

Right now she couldn't imagine a future without him, but that wasn't an option. "Yes, I guess I am."

Luke stared at her. "I don't believe this."

"I'm sorry," Vicky said miserably. "I thought you understood the situation."

"So did I, but obviously I didn't." He glowered fiercely. "Tell me something, Vicky. What exactly did you think we were doing here? Was I just a boy toy for you to experiment with?"

Vicky winced both at his harsh tone and at his equally harsh expression. "No, of course not. I thought we were having a...a fling."

"A fling?" Luke got to his feet. "That's all this was to you? A fling?"

"Yes," said Vicky. She rose as well and looked him straight in the eye. "That is all this is. And you shouldn't be surprised. You know the way it is for me. My parents—"

"I'm not talking about your parents. I'm talking about you and me."

"It's the same thing." She swallowed. "I can't help it. I let my family down before. I can't do it again. You, of all people, should understand. You're the one who is always spouting family values. Well, this is a value in my family."

"It is, is it?" Luke grabbed his jacket. "Well, if that's

all your family cares about, then I don't *want* to be part of it."

"Luke..."

"And if you're expecting me to find you a husband, you're out of luck because I won't do it." He stomped toward the door and yanked it open. "I'll be damned if I find a husband for the woman I love!"

"...AND THEN SHE TOLD me it was just a fling!" Luke said the next morning, concluding his story.

He sat in a chair in Barney's office, feeling more miserable and depressed than he had in his life. "I should have known better than to get involved with her in the first place."

"I don't know, Luke." Barney sat behind his desk, holding his head up with one hand, looking like the grim reaper with a headache. "I don't think she did anything that terrible."

Luke gave him a look of disgust. "You're supposed to be on my side!"

"I am on your side. I just think you're being too hard on Vicky. I mean, she didn't say she didn't care about you, did she?"

"No." She hadn't said that. And the way she'd looked at him—well, he'd been positive she'd felt the same way about him as he did about her.

"She didn't say she didn't *want* a future with you, either. She just said she couldn't."

"True, but—"

"You knew that when you went into it. She was real up front about it." A shadow passed over his face, making him look grimmer than ever. "Not like Suzy."

Luke decided Barney had enough problems of his

own and wandered back to his own office. Maybe Barney did have a point. Vicky had been up front about what she wanted in a man. He'd assumed she'd changed her mind—that she felt the same way about him as he felt about her. It turned out that superficial social things were more important to her than he was—and he should have known that.

He slapped open a folder. There were a good half-dozen cases sitting on his desk. Maybe if he immersed himself in his work he'd forget about Vicky and her perfect man.

Yeah, right. And maybe he'd forget his own name, too.

He was sitting at his desk, feeling mad at Vicky, furious with himself and disgusted with the world, when Barney stuck his head in the door. "Just because Vicky dumped you doesn't mean you're not on speaking terms with your phone."

Luke gave him a blank look. "What?"

Barney aimed his thumb in the direction of Luke's telephone. "Didn't you hear it ring? There's a cop on the line for you. Says he's got a lead on a guy with a tattoo."

"I'M FINE," Vicky insisted.

She wandered along the seabed simulators, comparing readings with the clipboard in her hand. "I admit I'm a little upset about the whole thing, but apart from that, I'm fine."

That was lie number three thousand; she was anything but fine. She'd been awake the entire night, alternating between being furious with Luke for being so difficult, and furious with herself for getting them both into this situation. Spread among those emotions was an aching emptiness that was worse than all the others.

Gina wasn't fooled. "A little upset?" she echoed. "You're more than a little upset, Vicky. You're majorly upset. You've taken the same readings twice, you've made mistakes writing them down, and a few minutes ago you were almost yelling at one of the techs because you misread the temperature chart."

Vicky flushed. "It was a mistake anyone could make."

"Not you." Gina put a hand on her arm. "Come on, Vicky. Why don't you do us all a favor, give Luke a call and see if you can patch it up?"

"Because I can't patch it up." Vicky sank into a chair and looked up at Gina. "It's unpatchable."

"Why?"

"You know why, Gina!" She dropped her forehead into a hand. "This is all my fault. I never should have hired Luke."

"No, you shouldn't have, but—"

"And I certainly shouldn't have had a fling with him." Vicky was thoroughly disgusted with herself. "I don't know what I was thinking. I should have known that I'm not the fling type."

"I don't believe there is a fling type, but—"

"I should have just kept looking for a husband by myself. I'm sure, sooner or later, I would have stumbled across one." She blinked back a lump in her throat. "Now I've made a mess of everything. Luke's furious, my parents are disappointed and I still don't have a husband." She glowered down at the clipboard. "And I'm so upset I can hardly concentrate on my vegetables!" Besides all that, she was terrified that the hole Luke had left in her life was never going to be filled.

"Maybe you should talk to him," Gina suggested. "He's had a little time to cool off. Maybe..."

Vicky's spirits rose at the suggestion. Then she remembered the bruised expression in Luke's eyes and shook her head. "No. It's better this way."

"Better?" Gina snorted. "There's no way this is better."

"It was going to end, anyway. It had to. Now it's over and done with and I can focus on doing what I'm supposed to be doing—finding the right man." She made a face at that idea. Right now it didn't appeal to her, but in a few days, she'd stop feeling like this. Then she could turn her attention to finding a husband. Of course, that wasn't going to be easy because now she didn't have Luke to help her.

"I think you're making a big mistake, Vicky. Luke's crazy about you. You're crazy about him." She shook her head. "Throwing that away is just nuts."

"You just don't understand," Vicky mumbled. No one understood. Not Gina. Not Luke. And not her parents, either.

"I'M TELLING YOU it's a waste of time," Barney grumbled.

He peered through the windshield at the few buildings that composed the Pike Retreat kennel. "There's no way a dog like Pumffy would hang around a place like this."

Privately Luke agreed with him. There were several upscale dog kennels around Miami, but this wasn't one of them. It was a run-down establishment with a dozen or so dog pens at the back. But a hunch was a hunch and it wouldn't hurt to check it out. Maybe he could get Barney's life back on track.

His own was a lost cause.

"It might not be. But according to Detective Henderson some woman called up, complaining about a guy trying to take her poodle. The guy claimed he found the animal outside her yard and was trying to put it back."

"So?"

"So the nanny for the Daniels told me the character who tried to take Munchkin had a tattoo on his arm. And the police told me he worked here."

"Why did the police tell you all this?" Barney asked.

Luke shrugged. He'd called his friends at the police station with the slight hope that maybe they knew something about dognappings in Miami. "They just like to keep me informed," he improvised. He put his hand on the door handle. "Let's do it."

"Luke..."

"Hey, it's better than sitting in the office and watching you look like the godfather in mourning." Luke opened the door. "How about if you go talk to them while I take a look around?"

"This is just dumb," Barney grumbled, but he obediently got out of the car and wandered toward the front.

Luke watched him for a moment, then slunk around to the back. There wasn't much to see—the dog pens were as rickety as the rest of the establishment and contained a bunch of mangy-looking animals that in no way resembled the classy Pumffy. Luke examined each one, then regretfully decided none of them could possibly be Pumffy, unless he'd had a nose job, a dye job and complete reconstruction of all his body parts. He took a quick peek into the storage shed, but there wasn't much to see in there—leashes, traveling cages, a few bags of dog food. Luke chuckled when he saw the Rothwell and Lewis Canine Excellence Dog Chow label on one bag. At least one of these critters had snooty taste in dog food.

That reminded him of Vicky's snooty taste in men, which just made him feel bad all over again.

He met Barney on his way back to the car. "There's just one guy in there and he doesn't know anything," Barney reported. "He didn't seem to care if we took a look around, either." He eyed Luke hopefully. "How about you? Did you see anything...suspicious?"

Luke started to shake his head, saw the flare of hope in Barney's eyes and changed his mind. "No, although I did see a bag of that dog food Pumffy likes so much."

"Anything else?"

This time Luke did shake his head. "I'm afraid not." He glanced around and caught sight of an old shed, sitting a hundred or so yards away from the house. "But I haven't checked in there yet."

"Don't bother," said Barney.

"It'll just take a minute." Luke ignored Barney's impatient sigh and headed for the structure. The building didn't look as if anyone had been there for a decade, if not longer, and it was almost impossible to see through the grimy windows. Luke gave it a swipe with his shirtsleeve and peered inside. For a moment he couldn't see anything. Then he did—a dozen dog kennels, containing a dozen disgusted-looking furry animals that were obviously used to much better quarters.

One of them, the most disgusted looking of the bunch, was a small, white animal that looked extremely familiar. Luke stared at him for a moment, then started to turn. "Hey, Barn—"

He stopped as he heard an unpleasant click in the vicinity of his right ear, and felt something cold pressed into the side of his head.

Great! He'd just found Pumffy and the dognapper!

He hoped Barney was suitably grateful.

12

"...SO I DECIDED TO TAKE a look at the dog food myself," Barney concluded. "Then I saw that guy trying to shove a gun up your neck, had a little scuffle with his partner and called the police from inside the house."

He sat on the couch in Luke's office, his feet stacked together on the coffee table, looking relaxed and happy, in spite of the bruise around his temple, which was almost as black as his suit. "I'd just taken out the character with the gun and was coming to let you out of the shed when the police arrived." He looked smug. "It turns out I was right. Those guys were stealing valuable dogs and using them for breeding purposes."

Luke was tired of the whole thing. "I know, Barn. I was there, remember?"

Barney kept going. "The police said it was a terrific piece of detective work. Of course, that's only to be expected, me being an ex-cop and all."

"I don't suppose you mentioned that I was the one who actually found the dog," Luke grumbled. He felt worse this morning than he had yesterday. While Barney was creeping around playing hero, he'd been locked up with a bunch of less than grateful canines. That had been followed by hours explaining it all to the police, and rounding up dogs. In spite of all that excitement he'd had a hard time falling asleep last night—

and when he did, his dreams were filled with images of Vicky with another man.

It wasn't the sort of thing that would put anyone in a good mood.

"Of course, I did." Barney looked pleased with himself. "And I told Suzy that, too. I thought it might make her feel a little more favorably toward you." He shook his head. "It didn't work. She's still mad at you."

Luke had lost part of the conversation. "Why would Suzy be mad at me? I found her dog for her."

Barney winced. "Yeah, well, uh, I told her what you'd said. About her taking the dog herself so her father would give her a trip to Europe." He looked up. "I didn't mean to tell her, Luke. She sort of...forced it out of me."

"Seduced it out of you, you mean," Luke guessed. Seduction made him think of Vicky, which made him wonder what she had been doing last night. Had she found some other guy—with the right credentials—to seduce? His misery increased.

"Whatever." Barney produced a rare ear-to-ear smile. "Let's just say she was real grateful Pumffy had been found."

"I guessed that." There had been a tearful scene last night when they'd returned the animal to the Harrises' home. Suzy had thrown her arms around Pumffy, and then around Barney. Luke had left when he'd realized they'd both forgotten he was there.

Barney started to rise, then sat back down. "By the way, you'd better start looking for a tux."

"A tux?" Luke blinked. "I found Suzy's dog so I have to get a tux?"

"For the wedding, idiot. If I have to wear one, you

have to wear one. Besides, you'll be best man." He frowned. "Of course, right now, Suzy doesn't want to even share the planet with you, much less a wedding ceremony, but after a while I'm sure she'll come around."

Luke raised a hand to scratch the back of his neck. "You and Suzy are getting married?"

"Yup."

"But...but I thought she was going to Europe."

"So did I," Barney admitted. "But it turns out she didn't want to go to Europe. She wanted me to tell her I wanted her to stay. That's why she was acting so peculiar about Pumffy. She was upset because I didn't." He shook his shaggy head. "Suzy's pretty clever, but sometimes she can be a little irrational." He passed a hand through his hair, looking both flummoxed and thrilled at the same time, and got to his feet. "I'd better get going. I'm meeting Suzy and her folks in an hour to start making the wedding plans."

"Suzy's parents know about this?"

"Uh-huh." Barney beamed. "They're a little stunned, but they don't seem too unhappy about it. Her father said it was going to save him a fortune in plane tickets. And her mother is so excited at the idea of planning a wedding that she can't think of anything else."

"That's great, Barn." It was too bad Vicky's parents wouldn't react that way to him. Of course, she hadn't been willing to give them a chance to do much, had she?

Barney took a couple of steps toward the door, then stopped and turned around. "Oh, by the way, I told Suzy how Vicky had broken up with you—sort of as a way to explain you saying all those nasty things about her. And you know what she said?"

Luke wasn't sure he was up to hearing this. "That it served me right?" he guessed.

"No. She said it didn't make any sense—because everyone has to have ancestors. How else could they be born?" He nodded his head. "She's darn clever, that Suzy."

Luke watched him float out of the room on his own personal cloud nine. Great. At least one of them had their life straightened out.

He got to his feet and wandered over to the window. He was really batting a hundred here. He'd completely misjudged the Pumffy situation—and Suzy, as well. He'd also misjudged Vicky. He'd thought she was a woman with the same values as he had, but she wasn't. She cared more about social prestige than anything, including him.

That wasn't quite fair. She did care about other things. Her work, for example. The world food shortage. Her family. There was no doubt she cared about her family.

He rested his forehead against the glass. Who was he trying to kid? Vicky wasn't a shallow socialite who was only interested in prestige and money. She was the woman he wanted, the woman of his dreams, and if she had said, "Screw my family," she wouldn't be herself.

It was just too bad he had to give her up because of some stupid accident of birth. Why couldn't he have a couple of well-connected relations in his background instead of...well, instead of whoever he had?

Luke froze. Maybe Suzy had a point. Everyone did have to have ancestors.

Luke grabbed his jacket off the sofa and started out the door. He'd spent all this time investigating other men's pasts, but he'd missed investigating the most important one of all.

His own.

"...AN ABSOLUTELY BRILLIANT piece of work," Dr. Lumbart praised. "You've made amazing progress, Vicky. We shouldn't have any problem ensuring that funding's available for the next century."

"I'm thrilled to hear that," Vicky murmured. No, she wasn't. She was miserable, but it had nothing to do with her research.

She wandered back to her office and stood in front of the window, staring out at the view. She'd once thought Miami was the most beautiful city in the world. Sure, it was lovely, but all those palm trees and greenery and ocean and sun got a little old after a while.

She turned away from it, muttering to herself. "Maybe I should go back to Boston. I could marry Harold, which would please mother no end."

She shuddered from her toes to her hair follicles. There was no way she could marry Harold, no matter how happy it would make her parents. She wasn't sure she could marry anyone who wasn't Luke.

Unfortunately, marrying Luke wasn't an option.

She returned to her desk. There she was, thinking about Luke again. How long was it going to take for her to get over him? It had been two days since he'd stomped out of her apartment and she was still so unhappy she could hardly concentrate on her work. She'd tried telling herself that it was for the best—that she didn't need to hang around with detectives from North Dakota who had a terrible effect on her behavior, but it hadn't helped. She'd tried telling herself that now she could concentrate on finding a husband who did meet all her qualifications, but she had no interest in doing that.

She swiveled to face her computer and banged at the switch to turn it on. She was tired of feeling this way. She was tired of her empty apartment, she was tired of being lonely and she was tired of missing Luke.

She was trying to make sense of the numbers on the screen when Gina came in. She stopped a few feet in front of Vicky's desk, a brightly clad figure dressed in yellow and black, and studied Vicky with concern. "How are you doing, Vicky?"

"I'm just fine," Vicky growled.

"Sure, you are. That's why you're looking so cheerful." She plunked a newspaper down on the desk. "Have you seen this?"

"Probably not." Vicky picked up the newspaper with little interest. "What is it? Is there an article in here about Oceanside?"

"Oceanside, no. Templeton and Adams Investigations, yes." Gina tapped a dark blue fingernail against a headline. "Luke's in the news."

"Luke?" Saying his name made her hurt all over again. "What's Luke doing in the newspaper?"

"He and his partner broke up some kind of dognapping ring." Gina's eyes sparkled with excitement. "It sounds just like the movies. There were guns and shooting and the police—"

"Shooting?" The paper fell from Vicky's hand as the world stopped turning. "Was anyone hurt?" She amended the question. "Was Luke hurt?"

"Not according to the paper." Gina scanned down the page. "It says that no one got injured except for one of the bad guys and all that happened to him was that he got bitten by a dog."

"Thank goodness." Vicky took a few breaths and then read the article. It sounded as if Luke had found that dog for Barney, after all. That was terrific. And even more terrific was that he hadn't been hurt.

"It's a shame he didn't fit your qualifications," said Gina. "He seems like a man any woman would want."

"He is," Vicky admitted. "He's everything a woman would want." A woman who wasn't her, that is.

"Then why aren't you with him? He did say that he's in love with you, didn't he?"

I'm not going to find a husband for the woman I love. "Yes, he did, but—"

"And you're in love with him." She paused. "You are in love with him, Vicky. You do know that, don't you?"

Vicky nodded. She hadn't framed it that way before, but she knew it was the truth. "Yes, I suppose I am, but—"

"So if he's in love with you and you're in love with him, why can't you two be together?"

Vicky blinked rapidly. "You don't understand. My parents—"

"Your parents!" Gina bounced out of her chair. "What is the matter with you people from Boston? Don't parents there care anything about their children?"

"Of course they do," Vicky defended, startled by the accusation. "My parents care about me."

"They have a funny way of showing it! My parents might just be from Nebraska, but they love me. They want me to be happy."

"My parents want me to be happy, too," Vicky insisted. They weren't the warmest people in the world, but they loved her. They wanted her happiness as much as anything.

"You're not happy now! You're miserable and depressed and hard to get along with."

Vicky bent her head. "I'll get over it."

"Sure, you will, in a year or two. But then what? Could you ever be happy married to someone who wasn't Luke?"

"Maybe." No, she couldn't. She couldn't be happy with Stephen or Emmett or any of those other men who were perfect. She could only be happy with Luke.

"Maybe you should give your parents a chance," Gina suggested. "You never know. It could be that they care more about you than they do about anything else."

Vicky watched her stroll out of the office. Gina was right! She was miserably unhappy without Luke. She wanted him back in her life. He'd said he loved her. She felt the same way. There was no reason why they couldn't be together, other than her parents. And her parents wouldn't want her to go through life feeling the way she'd felt these past two days. Besides, if she couldn't marry Luke she might not marry anyone. Then she'd never produce children. She didn't think her parents wanted that to happen, either.

She picked up the phone and dialed. "Hello,

Mother," she said when her mother answered. "It's Vicky. I'm calling to tell you that I've found someone."

Her mother's voice sparkled with delight. "You have?"

"Yes, I have. He's a detective from North Dakota and I love him and I intend to marry him."

There was dead silence on the other end of the line, followed by the thunk of the phone dropping to the floor. Vicky grimaced. It might take her parents a little time to get used to the idea, but she was sure they'd come around.

SHE DID LOOK old-fashioned in a black garter belt, Vicky decided a couple of days later. But it was a sexy, old-fashioned look—and she didn't do a bad job of filling out a bra. She just hoped Luke liked it.

She also hoped he wouldn't laugh in her face—or walk out of her life—when she showed it to him.

She stuffed a frozen vegetable entrée into the microwave for her to eat tonight. She wasn't planning on serving him a frozen dinner when she performed her seduction. She was going to make a great meal—even if she had to order it in. Perhaps it was a good thing that Luke wasn't going to be around for a few days. It would give her a chance to practice her culinary skills, and get used to walking around in this outfit.

She'd called this afternoon to talk to Luke, but he wasn't available. According to Barney, he was out of town on a case. She giggled as she recalled the conversation. Barney had recognized her voice right away and, before she could get out another word, had blurted out the information that Pumffy was safely at home and that he and Suzy were getting married. He sounded like a man drunk on happiness.

The only thing he hadn't been able to tell her was much about Luke. He just said something about Luke leaving town for a few days, and he'd let Luke know that she'd called as soon as he got back. "I hope it isn't anything dangerous," Vicky muttered to the microwave. "He'd better not get hurt before I pull my big seduction scene."

She frowned at that. Luke was fine. He was probably looking for a lost child, and he'd told her that seldom involved gunplay. On the other hand, there had been gunplay at that dognapping thing.

Chewing worriedly on her bottom lip, Vicky returned to the bedroom and started to remove her seduction outfit. She'd unsnapped a garter and had her hand on another when her doorbell rang. Vicky started for it, remembered she wasn't dressed for company and pulled her fuzzy flannel housecoat off the bed. "Who's there?" she called as she slid her hands into the sleeves.

"Luke."

Luke? Her mind went into a numbed panic. Luke was here? Why was Luke here? He was supposed to be out of town so she could get up enough nerve...

She gulped in a breath and opened the door. Luke loomed in the doorway, his expression unreadable behind his dark glasses. *I love you*, Vicky thought. "Hi," she said instead.

His eyebrows came down. "Are you alone?"

"Yes, I—"

"Good." He strolled into her hallway and tugged off

his glasses. "Does that mean you haven't found your perfect man yet?"

"N-not exactly." She had a million speeches practiced for this occasion. How come she couldn't think of anything to say? Of course, Luke could have made it easier by sticking to the script.

"No?" He patted her shoulder. "Well, don't worry about it. I think I've finally found him for you."

"You have?" He was really deviating from the script now. What had happened to not finding a man for the woman he loved? Had he decided he wasn't in love with her?

Luke wandered into the kitchen, sat down and pulled a bunch of papers from his inside pocket. "And let me tell you, it wasn't easy. I had to do more digging than I've done in my entire life." He glanced at the microwaved meal. "Do you have another one of those?"

"Yes, but—"

"Good." He got one from the freezer and shoved it into the microwave. "I've got a lot of material for you to go through and we might as well eat while we're doing it."

Vicky nervously chewed on a nail. She was going to serve him a vegetarian entrée dressed in nothing but a black garter belt—and if he laughed, she'd throw the entire foil packet at him.

Assuming they got that far. She rested her limp figure against the wall for support. "What, uh, sort of material do you have?"

"Husband material." He looked up, his face the picture of nonchalance, although his green eyes hinted at uncertainty. "You did hire me to find you a husband, didn't you?"

"Yes, I did but—"

"I did it." He spread papers across the table. "I think I've finally hunted down the perfect man."

Vicky folded her arms around herself. "I thought you said you wouldn't find me someone because you were in love with me yourself."

"I did say that, yes. But after I thought about it I realized I was putting you in a terrible position and that wasn't fair, so I—"

"So you what?" Vicky sat down. "Decided to find me another man, after all?" She wasn't sure if she was going to laugh or cry. "I know things are different in Miami but this is ridiculous."

"It's not—"

"Yes, it is." Vicky's voice rose. "You can forget the other man, Luke. I'm not going to marry anyone else when I'm in love with you!"

Luke winced. "This isn't going well, is it? If you'd just let me explain..." He stopped and blinked. "You're in love with me?"

"Yes, I am." Vicky took a breath. "And I had a wonderful seduction scene planned for when I told you that. Now I'm going to have to do it with microwave dinners." She got to her feet and yanked off her housecoat. "I don't know if I look sexy as hell in this outfit, but if you laugh..."

Luke's mouth dropped open. "I'm not going to laugh, honey." He got to his feet, his eyes never leaving her body as he moved. "I'm not even sure I can breathe." He grabbed her, hauled her up against him and wrapped his arms around her. "You're sexy as hell and I love you."

"Sure, you do," Vicky mumbled into his shoulder. "That's why you found me another man."

Luke kissed her ravenously, his tongue probing against hers while one of his hands closed around her breast. "I can explain about that."

Vicky wasn't in the mood for explanations. "I don't want you to explain, at least not right now. I want you to tell me that you love me and you want to marry me and spent the rest of your life with me."

"I love you and I want to marry you and spend the rest of my life with you." He pushed her a little way back so he could see into her face. His hand still rested possessively on her breast. "But what about your parents?"

Vicky tried to recall what parents were, but it was difficult with his thumb rasping across her nipple. "They'll get used to it."

"They don't have to get used to it. That's what I'm trying to tell you. I—"

"Tell me later," Vicky interrupted. She tugged at his belt, pushing his clothing away with eager fingers and took him in her hand. "Don't you think it's a little warm in here?"

Luke gave up. "Boiling," he agreed.

"So I TOLD MY PARENTS that if they loved me, they'd want me to be happy," Vicky concluded.

They lay in her bed, arms and legs entwined, facing each other. "I also told them that I wouldn't be happy with anyone but you."

"That's sweet." Luke kissed her forehead. "How did they take it?"

Her mother had dropped the phone and her father had told her he was calling a psychologist right away. "They're getting used to the idea. After I told them all about you, they were feeling a little better about it. Especially when I mentioned your commitment to—" she moaned as his hand stroked between her legs "—family values."

"Family values," Luke echoed. "Yeah. I've always been big on those."

"That's what I told them. It might take them a little while but they'll come around. They want me to be happy."

Luke pushed her onto her back and rolled on top of her. "They don't have to come around."

"Yes, they do, Luke. I'm not giving this up."

His eyes sparkled at her. "You might want to when you hear about the man I've found for you."

"I don't want—"

"He's a great guy," Luke pressed on. "Good looking. Great sense of humor. Clean fingernails. Not too athletic but enjoys the occasional game of tennis. Maybe not the most preferred career, but he does have social consciousness. And a degree. He's got a degree." He pressed a thigh between her legs. "Education is important, isn't it?"

"Very. But—"

"Best of all, he's got the bloodlines you want." He shifted sideways to face her. "Have you heard of a guy named John Adams?"

"Everyone's heard of John Adams, Luke. He's an icon in the history of—"

"His son's maid was pregnant when she got married." He put his lips against her ear. "Rumor has it that it was John Adams's son's child."

"Really?"

"Uh-huh. That child was my great-grandfather."

"Yours?" said Vicky. "You mean you're the man you found for me?"

"Yup. I've got all the qualifications you want in a man." He grinned down at her. "I told you I'd find you the perfect husband, didn't I?"

"Yes, you did," said Vicky.

"Well, I believe I've done it." He grinned and lowered his head. "Do you think we can mark the case closed now?"

Vicky pulled him down to her. "Definitely."

Take 2 bestselling love stories FREE

Plus get a FREE surprise gift!

Special Limited-Time Offer

Mail to Harlequin Reader Service®

P.O. Box 609
Fort Erie, Ontario
L2A 5X3

YES! Please send me 2 free Harlequin Temptation® novels and my free surprise gift. Then send me 4 brand-new novels every month, which I will receive before they appear in bookstores. Bill me at the low price of $3.57 each plus 25¢ delivery and GST.* That's the complete price, and a saving of over 10% off the cover prices—quite a bargain! I understand that accepting the books and gift places me under no obligation ever to buy any books. I can always return a shipment and cancel at any time. Even if I never buy another book from Harlequin, the 2 free books and the surprise gift are mine to keep forever.

342 HEN CH7H

Name	(PLEASE PRINT)	
Address	Apt. No.	
City	Province	Postal Code

This offer is limited to one order per household and not valid to present Harlequin Temptation® subscribers. *Terms and prices are subject to change without notice. Canadian residents will be charged applicable provincial taxes and GST.

CTEMP-98   ©1990 Harlequin Enterprises Limited

HARLEQUIN®
Temptation

It's a dating wasteland out there! So what's a girl to do when there's not a marriage-minded man in sight? Go hunting, of course.

Manhunting

Enjoy the hilarious antics of five intrepid heroines, determined to lead Mr. Right to the altar—whether he wants to go or not!

#669   *Manhunting in Memphis—*
Heather MacAllister (February 1998)

#673   *Manhunting in Manhattan—*
Carolyn Andrews (March 1998)

#677   *Manhunting in Montana—*
Vicki Lewis Thompson (April 1998)

#681   *Manhunting in Miami—*
Alyssa Dean (May 1998)

#685   *Manhunting in Mississippi—*
Stephanie Bond (June 1998)

She's got a plan—to find herself a man!

Available wherever Harlequin books are sold.

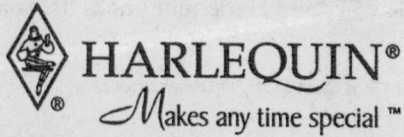

DEBBIE MACOMBER

invites you to the

HEART OF TEXAS

Join Debbie Macomber as she brings you the lives
and loves of the folks in the ranching community
of Promise, Texas.

If you loved Midnight Sons—don't miss
Heart of Texas! A brand-new six-book series
from Debbie Macomber.

Available in February 1998
at your favorite retail store.

Heart of Texas by Debbie Macomber

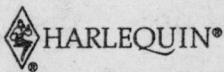

HARLEQUIN®

HPHRT1

MEN at WORK

All work and no play? Not these men!

April 1998

KNIGHT SPARKS by Mary Lynn Baxter

Sexy lawman Rance Knight made a career of arresting the bad guys. Somehow, though, he thought policewoman Carly Mitchum was framed. Once they'd uncovered the truth, could Rance let Carly go...or would he make a citizen's arrest?

May 1998

HOODWINKED by Diana Palmer

CEO Jake Edwards donned coveralls and went undercover as a mechanic to find the saboteur in his company. Nothing— or no one—would distract him, not even beautiful secretary Maureen Harris. Jake had to catch the thief—*and* the woman who'd stolen his heart!

June 1998

DEFYING GRAVITY by Rachel Lee

Tim O'Shaughnessy and his business partner, Liz Pennington, had always been close—but never *this* close. As the danger of their assignment escalated, so did their passion. When the job was over, could they ever go back to business as usual?

MEN AT WORK™

Available at your favorite retail outlet!

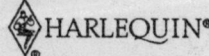 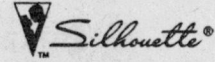

Look us up on-line at: http://www.romance.net

PMAW1

—with— Limited Edition CD

AN ALABAMA BOOK

And listen to Alabama sing their famous song on the free CD enclosed with the book!

Angels AMONG US

A hit song by one of country music's all-time great bands is now the inspiration for a heartwarming new book!

Angels Among Us features stories about people who, through their acts of kindness, have made the world a better place for all of us.

Don't miss your chance to pick up this beautiful hardcover (with special CD enclosed!), just in time for graduation and Mother's Day!

Available in May 1998 at your favorite retail outlet.

HARLEQUIN®
Makes any time special™

PBAMA

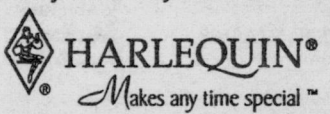

HARLEQUIN®
Temptation®

COMING NEXT MONTH